SECRETS OF THE CASTLETON MANOR LIBRARY™

A Novel Murder

Elizabeth Penney

Annie's®

AnniesFiction.com

Books in the Secrets of the Castleton Manor Library series

A Novel Murder
Bitter Words
The Grim Reader
A Deadly Chapter
An Autographed Mystery
Second Edition Death
A Crime Well Versed
A Murder Unscripted
Pride and Publishing
A Literary Offense
Up to Noir Good
For Letter or Worse
On Pens and Needles
Ink or Swim
Tell No Tales
Page Fright
A Fatal Yarn
Read Between the Crimes
From Fable to Grave
A Fateful Sentence
Cloak and Grammar
A Lost Clause
A Thorny Plot
A Scary Tale Wedding

Library of Congress-in-Publication Data
A Novel Murder / by Elizabeth Penney
p. cm.
I. Title
                        2016955471

AnniesFiction.com
(800) 282-6643
Secrets of the Castleton Manor Library™
Series Creator: Shari Lohner
Series Editors: Janice Tate and Ken Tate
Cover Illustrator: Bonnie Leick

10 11 12 13 14 | Printed in China | 9 8 7 6 5 4

Faith Newberry set a maple log on the burning nest of kindling and stood back to admire her work.

"Think that will do it, Watson?" she asked her black-and-white tuxedo cat, who watched with skeptical green eyes from his perch in an overstuffed armchair. "I haven't built a fire since, oh, Girl Scout camp." Flames began to lick the bark, and in a moment, the dry wood caught with a crackle.

Watson closed his eyes and began to purr, his highest endorsement.

"Glad you approve." With a laugh, Faith moved to the armchair and gently pushed Watson over so she could squeeze in beside him. Her tired muscles cried out in delight as she leaned back in the chair's plush embrace, stretching her sock-clad toes toward the heat. After spending the last two days packing and moving from Boston to Lighthouse Bay, a quaint village on Cape Cod, this was the first chance she'd had to relax.

This was also her first night in her new home, the cozy Victorian gardener's cottage located on the picturesque seaside estate of Castleton Manor. Often referred to as "the castle" by guests due to its imposing size and structure, Castleton Manor was a grand French Renaissance chateau-style mansion dedicated exclusively to literary events, book retreats, and vacationing book lovers who wished to get away from their hectic lives and enjoy the company of other literary aficionados. Each luxury suite in the twenty-nine-bedroom mansion was named after a famous literary figure and offered spectacular views of the manicured grounds and the ocean beyond.

The mansion held an impressive collection of books, and starting tomorrow, Faith would be the librarian and archivist for the unique venue. It was a librarian's dream job that oh-so-conveniently came with a dream cottage—at least in her eyes. This quaint stone cottage, nestled among the beautiful Victorian gardens, had so much more character than her former condo in Boston. And with the windows open, she could even hear the sounds of the ocean beyond the trees.

She glanced around the pretty room, enjoying the play of firelight dancing on polished antique furniture and the bright book covers filling the built-in bookcases on either side of the hearth. She leaned her head back and closed her eyes, allowing the warmth of the fire and the cat curled on her lap to lull her into a doze.

Rap! Rap! Rap!

Startled, Faith jerked awake, as did Watson, who jumped to the floor, using Faith's legs as a launching pad. "Ouch, Watson!" Rubbing her clawed knees, Faith tried to remember where she was. *Oh yes, the cottage at Castleton Manor.* That sound she heard was the lion's-head knocker banging against the front door.

Trying to avoid an irritated Watson, who wove between her legs and almost tripped her, Faith headed for the tiny foyer off the living room. *Who on earth would be visiting at this time of night?* Her aunt Eileen lived a few miles away on the edge of town, but she wouldn't come over without calling first. Regretting the lack of a peephole in the ancient wooden door, Faith took a deep breath and opened it.

"Good evening, Faith. Did I wake you?" Marlene Russell, the retreat's assistant manager and Faith's new boss, stood on the front step. Marlene's pointed nose twitched as her pale green eyes took Faith in, from stocking-clad feet to faded jeans to disheveled hair.

"Not at all. I was sitting in front of the fire." *Napping.* Faith brushed a hand through her long chestnut locks, attempting to straighten them. Marlene was apparently one of those women who, even at nine o'clock at night, was always immaculately turned out. She wore a long, cream-colored wool coat with tall brown leather boots, and her wavy blonde hair was pinned neatly in a bun. A buttery tan leather tote hung over her arm.

Marlene moved toward the threshold, obviously intent on entering the cottage. "I came by to make sure you were all set for tomorrow."

The Massachusetts Sherlock Holmes Society annual conference, a weeklong affair, was scheduled to start in the morning.

Faith stepped back to let Marlene inside and followed her into the living room. "Of course. I've been brushing up on Sir Arthur Conan Doyle's entire bibliography." With a pang of guilt, Faith eyed her paperback edition of *A Study in Scarlet*, the first Sherlock Holmes novel to be published, sitting on the end table. She had promised herself she would finish reading it tonight.

Marlene's thin brows rose. "Brushing up? I understood you were an expert in both British and American literature."

Faith flushed. Marlene hadn't been the one to choose her for the position, a last-minute vacancy, and since the moment they met, Faith had sensed the woman didn't approve of the hiring decision.

"As I told Mr. Jaxon," Faith said, careful to keep her voice pleasant, "those are my areas of specialty as a librarian. But before I give a lecture about any author, I always read their books again." Wolfe Jaxon, the eldest son and heir to the family's vast holdings, was also the general manager of the retreat, and Faith owed her job to him. Noticing the fire was dying down, she crossed the room to the fireplace to tend it.

Arms crossed, Marlene glanced around the room. "So are you settling in all right? The previous librarian had nothing but complaints about her *free* accommodations."

"Everything is perfect." Faith pushed aside the metal screen. "Is that why she left?"

Doris Lincoln had been the librarian-on-site before Faith. They'd both applied for the job some months before, but Doris beat her out in the last round of interviews. Faith had jumped at the chance when the call came six months later saying that the position was open again.

"I don't know. All Doris said was that she planned to travel and take a cruise around the world." Marlene snorted, a genteel little honk. "She certainly left us in the lurch."

The poker was missing from the set of tools, so Faith picked up the shovel and pushed at the log, trying to move it to a better spot. Watson came to sit on the hearthrug beside her, wide eyes fastened on Marlene with his tail, stumpy as it was, twitching. *Uh-oh. He doesn't care for her either.*

Nothing in life was perfect, Faith knew, and apparently that extended to dream jobs. "Well, I love the cottage. And I'll certainly do my best for you tomorrow." Faith forced a warm smile. "I'm looking forward to getting started."

"Make sure you come prepared," Marlene snapped. "The Sherlock Society is a tough crowd, and they'll expect you to know your stuff. You don't want to face their wrath." She gave a dramatic shudder.

Faith bit back a laugh as she imagined book lovers giving her a hard time, perhaps even heckling her. What would they do—throw rotten tomatoes? Magnifying glasses? Tweed caps? All highly doubtful. But from her experience as a librarian and archivist at Hawarden University, Faith knew that passions did run high when it came to rare books.

"Don't worry, Ms. Russell. I'll be prepared." Finished poking the log, Faith set the shovel back in the holder.

"All right then." Marlene's gaze darted around the room. "Is there anything you need tonight?" Her gaze landed on Watson, still sitting on the rug and regarding Marlene with disdain. "Oh yes. I forgot you had a pet." Her tone made it clear what she thought of that. "I hope he doesn't destroy the furniture. Why the Jaxons allow pets at the mansion—or the cottage—I'll never understand."

At this insult, Watson stood and arched his back. Faith bent to soothe him with a pat. "He's very well trained, I assure you."

"Hmm." Marlene pushed the handle of the bag higher on her shoulder. "I'll be on my way."

After the front door shut behind the manager, Faith bent to add another log to the fire. She had the feeling she wouldn't be going to bed early after all. She really should review her research again to be doubly sure her first lecture was a resounding success.

The cat purred loudly, but his human was deeply engrossed in her reading. He jumped from the back of the couch and half snuggled, half collapsed in a small furry heap by her side, but she hardly noticed. He tried to slip beneath the book and into her lap, but after the briefest of ear scratches, she pushed him back to her side and the edge of the sofa.

Humph! And after he had tried to warn her about that other human. She was nothing but trouble. He could feel it down to his claws.

Impassively and regally, he slunk away from his human and back to the hearthrug. He was too proud to pout, so he groomed himself in the glow of the fireplace. It wouldn't be long before she would be off to bed. Would it?

Faith's prediction about staying up late was correct, and as a consequence, seven came far too soon. Hearing Watson's early-morning "I want breakfast" cry, she opened one eye. He was sitting right next to her on the bed, his nose only an inch from hers.

She laughed and sat up. "Don't worry, I'm awake." It had been fourteen years since Faith had rescued him as a kitten from behind a snow-covered dumpster outside her apartment. Watson had lost most of his tail either due to an accident or to the frigid Massachusetts weather. Faith had named him Watson because she loved Sherlock Holmes mysteries. Sometimes she called him "Rumpy" in reference to his stubby tail. He preferred Watson, or at least that's what Faith had come to believe. Through the years they had developed a set of very specific daily rituals. Feeding Watson first thing, before she'd even had a single drop of coffee, was one of them.

In the morning sunlight Faith admired the cozy bedroom, one of two in the cottage. This one was at the back, overlooking woods through tall lattice-paned windows. The furniture was simple, a four-post walnut bed with matching dresser and wardrobe. She adored living here already.

"I hope I make it through today," she told Watson, throwing back the covers. "Or else you and I will be living with Mom." The cat squalled in response and bolted toward the kitchen.

Faith found a pair of slippers and shuffled after him. At age thirty-nine, moving back into her childhood home with her mother, who lived less than two hours away, was truly an option of last resort. The very idea of it was enough of a blow to her pride to motivate her to succeed in her new position. "Despite whatever Marlene Russell throws at me," she muttered under her breath.

Two hours later, dressed in a black suit with a cream blouse, Faith headed through the Victorian gardens toward the mansion, hands clammy and heart thumping with first-day jitters. Even now, in autumn, the gardens were lush and lovely. Realizing she was behind schedule, she sped up, skirting a still-fragrant herbal knot garden and bursting through an opening in a tall topiary hedge.

Bam!

She ran full tilt into a tall, dense body and almost fell back onto her seat.

"Steady there, my dear." Strong hands gripped her shoulders.

Faith stared up at the man in amazement. She had literally bumped into Sherlock Holmes. He had a beak-nosed face, a large chin, and piercing eyes. A tweed deerstalker cap sat on his head, and a tan-and-black plaid cape covered his shoulders.

The man chuckled. "Yes, the resemblance is uncanny, isn't it? I'm Benedict Sinclaire, and obviously I have a Sherlock problem." He released her.

"Nice to meet you. I'm Faith Newberry, librarian here at Castleton." A yip caught her attention, and she glanced down. A brown miniature dachshund stood at the man's feet, also dressed in a tiny matching cape. "Oh, how sweet. Is that your dog?"

Benedict scooped up the ball of fur. "Yes, this is Molly." Molly and Faith regarded each other solemnly for a moment, then Molly began to squirm and bark. Startled, Benedict released her, glancing over Faith's shoulder. "Oh, so that's what's got her going."

Faith turned to see Watson sitting in the break in the hedge. "That's my cat, Watson. He was supposed to stay home today."

"Watson, heh?" Benedict grinned. "Good name choice."

Molly dashed toward Watson, and Watson turned and ran. The costumed dog took chase, and Benedict hurried to catch up to the dog, his cape billowing behind him in the breeze. The three of them racing across the lawn were a comical sight. "Don't worry, Faith," he called over his shoulder, "she only wants to make friends."

Watson could outrun—and certainly outclimb—any dog, so Faith wasn't worried a bit. Shaking her head in amusement, she continued on toward the imposing stone mansion, now visible through the trees. Every time she saw the place, her breath caught in her chest. She hadn't seen a private residence so extravagant and gorgeous outside of Newport, Rhode Island. The sixty-thousand-square-foot chateau-style mansion, built in 1895, was a very visible symbol of the Jaxon family wealth, amassed from a vast shipping empire that was started centuries ago.

And if the legend is true, they came by some of their riches by cheating my Newberry ancestor out of his. Faith sighed at her foolishness at even remembering the tattered old tale that swirled around the mysterious death of Josiah Newberry on a Jaxon-owned ship in the early 1800s.

As though summoned by her thoughts of Jaxon wealth, she spotted Wolfe Jaxon's dark blue BMW sedan parked among the employee vehicles. A shiver of excitement tingled at the realization that the handsome, forty-four-year-old Jaxon heir was in residence. As the owner and general manager of Castleton Manor, he reserved the entire third floor of the mansion for his personal use.

She had only met him once, when interviewing with him and his mother, Charlotte, but he'd made an indelible impression. Tall, suave, and charismatic, he would have made a prime candidate for one of those millionaire bachelor television shows—or so Faith thought. *Steady now, Faith.* When she was ready to date again, she doubted it would be with someone so obviously out of her income bracket.

Huge double doors in the front of the mansion led into the Main Hall, and Faith paused to get her bearings. From the brief tour she'd taken during her interview, she knew the library was to the left . . . somewhere.

"Are you lost?" A perky blonde woman who looked to be in her early thirties strode toward Faith, footsteps ringing on the marble floor.

"Actually, I might be. I'm Faith Newberry, the new librarian."

The woman extended her hand with a beaming smile and shook Faith's. "Awesome. I'm Brooke Milner, sous-chef. I'm responsible for some of the more, ah, *creative* dishes we serve here." She gestured. "Follow me. I'll show you to the library."

"Thank you. I've been here once, and all I recall is that it's huge." As they proceeded past the cantilevered marble staircase and into the two-story gallery, Faith stared around in awe. Everything was exquisite. She couldn't hold back a gasp or two.

"I know. I'm still getting used to it myself," Brooke said, "and I've been here five years."

Five years. Faith tucked away that information. If Brooke was as nice as she seemed, maybe she could provide the inside scoop on why Doris Lincoln left so soon after starting the job. And perhaps provide a little information on Wolfe Jaxon as well.

"Here we are." Brooke peered into the library. "It looks like your class is here already."

Brooke was right; about two dozen men and women were in the room, chatting in small groups or browsing the shelves. A few even had dogs at their feet or cats on their laps, Faith noticed with pleasure. Maybe she could bring Watson with her to work. The room itself was spectacular, with a carved walnut ceiling and woodwork, red velvet furniture, and two-story built-in bookcases holding literally thousands of volumes. Small locked glass cases held some of the collection's rare volumes. Faith had been given a set of keys with the warning to guard them zealously.

Faith took a deep breath, steeling herself to go in and face the group. "Thanks, Brooke. It was nice to meet you."

Brooke grinned. "Same here. Maybe I'll see you at lunch." With a wave, she darted down the corridor.

Faith stepped inside the grand room. "Hello, everyone," she called. "I'm Faith Newberry, the librarian here at Castleton Manor."

As always, once Faith launched into her lecture, her nerves eased, and she began to enjoy herself. It helped enormously that the guests were so interested in the topic of first-edition Sherlock Holmes novels. While she spoke, the crowd grew to include Benedict Sinclaire, the man she'd met in the garden; his dog, Molly; and the assistant manager, Marlene, who watched her with icy eyes and crossed arms.

"We are most fortunate here at Castleton," Faith said, reaching into her bag for the set of keys, "to have the very first Sherlock Holmes novel ever printed in book format." To the gasps and murmurs of the group, she unlocked the glass case holding the first printing of *A Study in Scarlet*. "There are very few originals still in existence."

Benedict Sinclaire gave a big sigh. "I've always coveted a copy for my collection of firsts."

Marlene pushed her way through the group, her own key ring jingling at her waist. "Should you be handling that?" she whispered harshly.

"I know what I'm doing," Faith said through a tight smile, pulling on a pair of cotton gloves and gently picking up the book. "Ladies and gentlemen, you must always wear gloves when handling rare books..." Her voice trailed off as shock iced her spine. Even through the gloves, she could tell the book was a fake. It felt wrong, flimsy in weight. It even smelled wrong, not like old paper and ink but like nothing at all. With a huge effort, she gathered her wits and continued as if nothing were wrong, "There are certain features that tell you which edition you're holding..."

Somehow Faith made it through the rest of her lecture without revealing the horrible truth about the supposed first edition. Had someone replaced the real book unbeknownst to the Jaxon family, or did the owners know the volume was fraudulent—a lie they told the public to lure unsuspecting book lovers to their expensive retreat? Either way, revealing the truth was going to cause turmoil.

My dream job just turned into a nightmare.

Wolfe Jaxon approached her after the listeners dispersed while Faith was busy locking the case that held the forged book.

"Nice job, Miss Newberry," he said in a deep, resonant voice, his blue eyes crinkling when he smiled. "I think we made the right choice for our new librarian."

"Good morning, Mr. Jaxon. I certainly hope to prove you right." Though her nerves were frazzled, Faith instinctively smiled up at him, a barrage of thoughts and sensations jostling for her attention. *Does he know about the book? Does he wonder if I know? Gosh, he's attractive.*

Wolfe wore a tailored suit and dress shirt with tie, a little formal for everyday wear, but it worked on him.

A guest appeared next to them with a question, so Wolfe nodded and gave her a small salute. "I'll let you get back to work. Feel free to call me if you need anything."

Anything . . . like the police or a rare book expert? Faith tamped down her unease and focused on the woman seeking her attention.

After closing the library for lunch, she rushed through the gardens to the cottage. She needed a cup of hot tea and some Watson time. Then she'd call her aunt Eileen and seek her advice about the book. Eileen, also a librarian, would surely know what to do.

She reached the cottage to find Watson digging under one of the hydrangea bushes, both front paws churning away as dirt flew.

"Watson! What are you doing? Stop that!" Faith raced to stop him from tearing up the garden, which was no doubt on Marlene's no-no list.

She lifted the protesting, flailing cat away from the dirt hole, wondering what he was so intent on uncovering.

Then she saw it. An orange leather purse strap poking out of the dirt. Faith set Watson down and grabbed it. After a few tugs, the bag came up out of the ground. *Why on earth would someone bury a purse? Especially one this nice.* Even smeared with earth and dead leaves, it was obviously high-quality leather, perhaps even handmade.

Faith unzipped the top, jerking on the tag a few times to loosen dirt clogging the zipper. The designer label read, *Donatello.* Not a brand she'd ever heard of, but that didn't mean anything considering she often purchased her purses at big-box stores that also sold cat food. Inside the purse, she found a wallet, a set of car keys, lipstick, a pack of tissues, and a hairbrush.

Curious, she unsnapped the wallet. The driver's license picture showed an attractive older woman. *Doris Lincoln.*

Dismay coiled in Faith's stomach as she studied the photo. *This makes no sense.* Worried, Faith looked at the purse again and then at Watson, who merely turned and sauntered away with what appeared to Faith to be a satisfied strut.

2

Faith searched through the purse, unzipping each little pocket and reaching her hand inside. She could think of no logical reason why Doris Lincoln would leave Castleton Manor without taking her purse. Especially if the former librarian planned to travel around the world, as Marlene had said. The woman would surely need her ID . . . her credit cards . . . her keys . . .

Dread sat heavy in Faith's stomach as she remembered other cases of missing women she'd heard about. Without exception, personal belongings left behind meant foul play.

Watson strolled over and wound his way around her legs, meowing.

"I know, Watson. There's something very wrong with this picture." Faith set down the orange purse and dug around for her cell phone. She needed to call Marlene and report what she'd discovered.

Faith was pouring boiling water into a teapot in the kitchen when Marlene finally arrived, her presence announced by a rapping on the front door. When Faith opened it, she was surprised to see Wolfe standing behind Marlene.

"I thought I'd come along and find out what's going on," Wolfe said. "It sounded strange."

Marlene clucked. "I'll say." She put both hands on her hips, clad today in a burgundy wool skirt suit. "Where's this purse that supposedly belongs to Doris?"

"It's in the kitchen." Faith gestured. "Follow me."

Faith had set the dirty purse on a piece of newspaper on an otherwise empty counter. She found her gloves in her pockets and slid them on.

"Why are you doing that?" Marlene asked, her eyes narrowing. "Afraid to get your hands dirty?"

"No." Faith pulled out the wallet. "I don't want to mess up any fingerprints that might be on this more than I already have." She showed both of them the license. "See? It says, *Doris Lincoln.*"

Wolfe studied the license. "Where did you say you found it?"

"Under a bush outside. My cat dug it up." The animal in question jumped up onto one of the oak kitchen chairs and began to lick his paw.

Marlene's lip curled at the sight. "Maybe Doris misplaced it and couldn't wait around to find it before she left."

"That wouldn't explain how it got buried in the garden." Faith shook her head. "I think foul play is involved."

The assistant manager clapped a hand to her forehead. "Foul play? That's ridiculous. We're not living in a mystery novel here. I can't have you going around making such absurd accusations! You're new here! What would you even know ab—"

"Marlene." Wolfe's tone was sharp. "Calm down."

"Morbid stories like this could seriously damage Castleton's reputation," Marlene sputtered before grumbling into silence.

"Let me worry about that." Wolfe's gaze was somber when his eyes met Faith's. "Call the police."

Marlene insisted on returning to the mansion once the call was made so she could get a head start on any "damage control" that might be necessary due to the sight of police presence on the property. Faith was left alone to entertain Wolfe while waiting for the officer to arrive. The Lighthouse Bay dispatcher promised it wouldn't be long. At Faith's invitation, Wolfe sat at the kitchen table next to Watson.

"Would you like a cup of tea, Mr. Jaxon?" Faith opened the cupboard to pull out mugs, wrestling with whether or not to bring up the counterfeit Sherlock Holmes book. *What if I'm wrong about it? Maybe I should look at it again. And then talk to Aunt Eileen.*

"Please call me Wolfe. We're fairly informal around Castleton." He reached out a hand and gently stroked Watson's head. "I'd love a cup, as long as it isn't that herbal stuff. It always tastes like boiled sticks to me." Watson tolerated the attention for a moment, then jumped down and stalked into the other room.

"Okay, Wolfe. And I'm Faith, as you know." She laughed nervously, still not entirely comfortable with her new boss. "No herbal tea here. It's fully caffeinated English." She set two mugs on the table and filled them with steaming liquid. Fortunately, she managed to control the shaking of the hand holding the teapot. Not only was she reeling from discovering the forged book, but now there was the mystery of Doris's purse. She had a really bad feeling about the entire situation.

"English tea, huh? Have you been across the pond?"

Faith picked up her mug, enjoying the warmth as she cradled it in her hands. "Yes. I studied two semesters abroad." She shrugged. "I figured if I was going to become an expert on English literature and history, I needed to go there."

"Good point. I travel to London frequently on business. Hate the weather, love the ambiance."

"Agreed." They drank in silence for a minute, Faith racking her brain about what to say. Besides the fact that he was the head of the retreat center and drop-dead gorgeous as well, every time she glanced at the purse, she felt a surge of anxiety. *When will the police get here to take a report?* It appeared a lost pocketbook wasn't a high priority.

Wolfe was quiet too, and he also kept shooting glances at the purse. They both gave sighs of relief when someone finally rapped on the front door.

"Fancy meeting you here," Brooke said as she arrived at the front door of Snickerdoodles Bakery and Tea Shop at the same time as Faith. The sous-chef had changed out of her uniform and into jeans, boots, a sweater, and a peacoat. "I always stop here before going to the book club meeting."

Faith pointed to the two-story stone Colonial building next door to the bakery. "You mean the book club that meets at the Candle House Library? That's where I'm headed. My aunt is the librarian there. She invited me to join tonight's meeting but suggested I stop in here first."

Brooke's eyes widened. "Your aunt is Eileen Piper?" She opened the door for Faith to enter, the bells jingling above. "I had no idea! I guess a love of books runs in your family."

"It sure does." Faith stepped into a large square room with small tables and chairs in the front and glass cases holding treats at the back. The place was empty except for two middle-aged women seated at a table and a plump, red-haired woman working behind the counter. Faith inhaled scents of vanilla, cinnamon, chocolate, and brewing coffee. "Wow. I can see why you like to come here."

"It's the best bakery in town. And I should know, right? Being in the food business and all." Taller in her heeled boots, Brooke sashayed toward the counter. "Hey, Jane. What's good tonight?"

The redhead behind the counter glanced up, a wide smile on her freckled face. "Everything. But I might try the custard-filled cream puffs."

"Cream puffs? Oh my."

Faith edged closer and peered into the case. Fat pastry puffs oozing yellow cream sat on a tray, begging to be devoured. "I'll take one."

"We'll take four," Brooke corrected. "I'm ordering for Eileen and Midge too. Midge is our other book club member," she said to Faith.

Jane pulled on plastic gloves and cast a glance at Faith. "I haven't seen you around. New to town?"

"I'm Faith Newberry, the new librarian at Castleton Manor." Out of the corner of her eye, Faith saw the two customers turn to stare, obviously listening. Then they bent close and began to whisper, darting glances at her. Apparently her arrival was big news in the tiny town.

The baker nodded. "Glad to meet you. I'm Jane McGee."

"The best baker on Cape Cod," Brooke added.

"I'll let you judge for yourself," Jane said, setting cream puffs carefully inside a box. She closed the lid. "Enjoy."

When Brooke and Faith entered the town's historic library next door, Eileen Piper raced around the corner of her desk and gave Faith a huge hug. "I'm so glad to have you living in Lighthouse Bay!" Petite, with shoulder-length brown hair and sparkling blue eyes, the sixty-two-year-old librarian and grandmother was a bundle of energy and enthusiasm.

Faith hugged her back, enjoying the comfort of her favorite aunt's touch. "I'm glad to be here. Well, I was, until today."

"That sounds ominous." Eileen took Faith's arm. "Let's go into the reading room."

The cozy room off the main library area held rocking chairs, armchairs, and a sofa along with conveniently placed lamps and tables. All were strategically situated to have a view of the massive fireplace once used to melt tallow when the eighteenth-century building served as a small candle factory.

A woman sitting in a rocker rose as the trio entered. Of medium height and weight, she had shoulder-length blonde hair and green eyes. "Hey, I'm Midge Foster." She had a slight Southern accent, barely enough to add a lilt. "You must be Eileen's niece." She pointed with a polished red fingernail to the tiny Chihuahua lying at her feet. "And this little old thing is Atticus." The dog wore an orange hat with a big pom-pom and a matching sweater.

"I'm Faith, and if I'd known pets were welcome, I would have brought my cat." It seemed people in Lighthouse Bay took their pets everywhere.

"Midge is the concierge vet for Castleton Manor," Brooke said as she set down the drink tray on a center table and took a cup.

Faith set the pastry box beside it and opened the lid and asked, "So you make house calls?" She was amazed at this news. She didn't think vets did that anymore.

Midge nodded. "I'll be up there this week to see a Miss Molly Sinclaire." She selected a cream puff. "I also own Happy Tails, the gourmet pet treat bakery across the street. We bake up delicious, healthy treats . . . but nothing this decadent."

After everyone settled in with refreshments, Eileen turned to Faith. "Usually we discuss the book we're all reading before we socialize . . ."

As if on cue, Brooke held up the selection, a Mary Russell-Sherlock Holmes mystery by Laurie King.

Eileen continued, "But I want to hear about what happened to spoil your first day in that magnificent library at Castleton. What I wouldn't give for their collection."

Midge, apparently sensing Faith's reluctance, made a zipping movement across her lips. "Anything that's said in the Candle House Book Club stays in the book club."

Faith studied the circle of concerned faces. Sensing she could trust Brooke and Midge—Eileen was a given—she decided to get everything off her chest. Well, almost everything. She still wanted to discuss the fake first-edition book with her aunt in private, and there'd been no time to bring it up on the phone.

"Well, as odd as it sounds, my cat dug up a purse belonging to Doris Lincoln today." She went on to tell the tale, as well as her encounter with the by-the-book young police officer Bryan Laddy.

At his name, Brooke gave a little squeal, exclaiming about the tall, dark-haired officer's good looks.

"He may be attractive, but I've never met anyone so skeptical," Faith said. "He doubted every word I said. I almost felt like he thought *I* buried the purse."

"The whole thing is really strange. How could Doris go on a world cruise without her wallet?" Eileen propped one hand in her chin thinking. "Does anyone know when she left the area?"

"Labor Day weekend," Brooke said. "She was at Castleton on

Saturday and not there on Tuesday when most of us got back. The retreat was closed Sunday and Monday."

"Peter and I were out of town visiting the kids, so I'm no help there," Midge said.

"I was here that weekend, remember, Aunt Eileen?" Faith asked. "We had a lobster lunch as a good-bye to summer." Dread knotted her stomach. "I think something awful might have happened to Doris."

Eileen reached over and patted her knee. "Let's hope not. At least it's in the hands of the police now."

Fifteen minutes before closing the library at Castleton Manor the next day, a retreat guest wearing a deerstalker cap stepped into the library and stared around at the empty room in confusion. This was the fifth person Faith had seen in such attire—and the first woman. The rest of her outfit was from the Victorian era, a long, sweeping skirt and a nipped-in jacket. Sherlock fans took their admiration for the detective very seriously, Faith was learning. A shaggy Irish wolfhound trotted at the woman's heels.

"May I help you?" Faith asked, rising from the tall stool behind the desk. Watson lay curled near her feet, a spot he rotated to along with the velvet bench in front of the fireplace and a window seat in the second-floor gallery. His first day at the library had gone well, and Faith enjoyed having him there. His presence had helped to calm her nerves as she'd secretly examined the Sherlock Holmes book in question again. As best she could tell, it was indeed a fake. But she still hadn't decided what to do about it.

The woman strode to the desk and handed Faith the daily calendar page. "I can't figure out where my lecture is being held." She pointed to *Women in Sherlock's World*, listed along with *What Would Sherlock Do? Presenting a Case from Today* and *Sherlock in Film: The Silent Era.* Each had a room designation.

The wolfhound thrust his big nose under the desk, and Watson edged onto Faith's foot.

"Let's check the map." Faith placed the laminated mansion map on the desk so both she and the woman could see it.

The wolfhound got onto his belly and tried to insert his entire body into the small slot available under the desk. Watson hissed and swiped at the dog's nose. The dog howled and bucked upward, jostling the desk.

"Clancy. Get out from under there," the woman ordered.

Faith reached down and nudged the cat backward. All she needed was for her cat to injure a guest's animal. At the dog's second howl, Watson bolted for the gallery stairs.

"I'm so sorry about that." Faith turned to glare at Watson, but he was nowhere in sight.

The woman pulled her dog out from under the desk and examined his nose. "It's fine. I think he was more freaked out than hurt." She patted the dog and stood. "Now that the excitement's over, let's find out where my lecture is."

Once Faith sent the woman and her dog on their way, she realized it was past closing time. Fortunately no other browsers were in the library, so it was only a matter of turning the hanging sign to Closed and locking the door. Then she went around and dimmed the lights, leaving only the one on the desk illuminated.

She gathered her belongings, eager to go back to the cottage, put her feet up, and drink a cup of tea in front of the fire. The second day at the manor had sped by, and she'd barely had a chance to think about the orange purse planted in the garden.

"Watson," she called. "Where are you? *Rumpy!*" The second name was her pet name for the short-tailed cat. She circled the room, checking behind furniture and curtains. *He must be upstairs.* She climbed up to the gallery level and searched thoroughly there, calling his name every few minutes.

"Come on, Watson. It's time to go home." Hopefully he hadn't managed to sneak out to the hall. If he had, he could be anywhere in the vast building. Three stories and a basement . . . there was no telling where a curious cat might hide. Faith sighed, her shoulders slumping, the vision of hot tea by her own fireside quickly fading.

She clumped down the stairs to the main floor of the library. As she was walking past the fireplace area, she heard a faint meow.

"Watson?" She checked all the furniture, looking behind the cushions and kneeling down to peer underneath. No cat.

The mew came again, from the direction of the wall. Faith stared at it, confused. *Has he somehow gotten behind one of the bookcases? But how could that be?* They were built in.

Faith pressed her ear against the paneling near a hanging tapestry. "Come on, meow for me, Rumpy." He obligingly did.

That little rascal is *behind the wall!* Faith ran for her cell phone. There was only one person she knew who could help with this problem. The man who grew up in the castle. Wolfe Jaxon.

The cat sniffed at the wall. His human sounded upset, which meant she needed him badly. Normally he wouldn't deign to respond to the ridiculous nickname she'd made up for him—Rumpy.

He didn't like what it implied about his figure or his lack of tail. But he knew this was serious. Rising up on his hindquarters, he called to her and pawed at the stone. No luck. The entrance was sealed.

Blinking, he looked around. It was pitch-dark, so dark that even his excellent feline eyesight was nearly useless.

That left his nose as his best weapon. He twitched his whiskers, trying to detect a whiff of fresh air, a clue to another exit. Then he smelled something strange, something even more offensive than dog's breath. It wasn't the dust or mice or spiderwebs. It was something . . . very bad.

"You're sure he's behind the wall?" Wolfe asked. Faith had obviously interrupted him relaxing, since his shirtsleeves were rolled up and his tie was missing.

"Positive." Faith rapped on the wall. "Watson. Talk to me." Obligingly, the cat complied. "See? How is this possible? Are there secret rooms in this place?"

"Old servants' passageways. Hold on a minute while I remember how to do this." He cast Faith a disarming smile. "It's been decades. My brothers and I used to love exploring them when we were kids. The mansion is full of hidden halls, doorways, and access points." He went to the tapestry, pushed it aside, and fiddled with the carved paneling near the floor of his ancestral home.

The wall slid aside, and Wolfe quickly put his shoulder into the opening. "If you don't move fast, it will shut again."

"That must be what happened to Watson." Faith stepped through the gap, wrinkling her nose as a foul smell assaulted it. "I can't see a thing."

Wolfe turned on his phone flashlight and beamed the light around the space, a stone alcove extending into the dark.

Faith saw the high-heeled shoes first, lying on the floor about ten feet away. As the narrow shaft of light rested on them, she realized something horrible.

They still contained feet.

3

Faith screamed. "Oh, Wolfe! There's something awful in here!"

He moved forward, casting the light around the alcove, on the walls and ceiling. "What is it, a dead mouse?"

"Not exactly." Faith wrapped her arms around herself, shivering. "Shine the light to the left again. Look for the shoes."

"Shoes? What do you mean, shoes?" Wolfe obeyed, sounding puzzled. Then he glimpsed the high heels. "Wait here, Faith. Don't move." He stepped farther into the inky alcove, the pinpoint of light moving with him.

Soft darkness closed around Faith and she resolutely kept her eyes on the sliver of light framing the exit into the library. *My lifeline out of here.* Behind her, Wolfe exclaimed when he reached what Faith knew was a body. The creeping certainty up her spine only confirmed what her intuition told her. But maybe she was wrong. Maybe it had been there a century or so . . . but in those stilettos? Not likely.

"It's Doris Lincoln," Wolfe said.

She hadn't heard him approach and she gasped at his words, which now sank in. "It is Doris? Then she didn't go on a cruise after all."

"Apparently not." Wolfe took her arm, guiding her toward the opening. "Come on, let's get you out of here. I need to call the police."

Out in the warm safety of the library, Wolfe settled Faith on the red velvet settee and found a chair to hold the entrance to the secret room open. Then he went to the desk to place the call. Watson jumped up beside Faith and she gathered him into her lap, where he snuggled. He always seemed to sense when she was upset and tried to comfort her; it was one of his most endearing traits.

And oh, was she ever upset. The woman she replaced was lying in an alcove behind the library wall. Had she gone back there to do something and been trapped? Faith imagined her calling for help and no one coming to her rescue. How dreadfully sad and tragic.

Still holding the receiver, Wolfe said, "They'll be here right away." He pressed buttons again. "Marlene? I need you in the library. The police are on their way, but I'm having them come to the side terrace entrance, not the front door." Squawking erupted. After a few seconds, he cut her off. "I'll tell you when you get here." After setting down the receiver, he strode across the room toward Faith. "Do you need anything? Something to eat or drink perhaps?"

Faith shook her head, her stomach rebelling at the thought of consuming anything. At this moment, she thought she might never eat again.

"Let me know if you change your mind." Wolfe went to the library door, testing the handle. "Good, it's locked. The last thing we need is to be inundated with curious onlookers." He paced about the carpet, hands clasped behind his back, stopping now and then to peer out the French doors toward the parking lot. "I asked them to be discreet, to come to this side instead of the front."

All was silent in the library, sounds from the main house muffled by its secluded location and insulating shelves of books. At this hour, evening activities had begun. Faith imagined the happy chatter of guests mingling in the Great Hall, while in the kitchen, a frenzy of meal preparations were under way. The agenda tonight included a social hour followed by an opening-night dinner featuring locally caught seafood, with chicken and vegetarian options. How Faith wished she could be with them, blessedly ignorant of the tragedy in the library.

"Ah. They're here." Wolfe unlocked the French door and opened it. "Come on in, Chief."

Faith raised her head at the entrance of a tall man with sharp blue eyes and a military bearing. Bryan Laddy, the officer she had met earlier, followed his boss into the room.

The chief's eyes fastened on Faith as he strode across the carpet. "Who's this?" Although alert with authority and intelligence, he also projected an air of calm kindness. "I'm Chief Garris. Andy Garris."

Faith stood. "I'm Faith Newberry, the new librarian." She nodded at Bryan. "I've already met Officer Laddy."

"That's right, Chief," Laddy said. "Remember the call about the buried purse? Miss Newberry found it."

"You've had quite a welcome to Lighthouse Bay." Garris cocked his head. "What's this, your second day on the job?"

"That's right." Faith was amazed. Garris must have had his fingers on the pulse of everything that happened in Lighthouse Bay. Well, almost everything. He hadn't known Doris Lincoln was still in town.

"Faith was with me when I discovered Ms. Lincoln's body," Wolfe said. "Her cat was trapped behind this wall."

The chief finished taking Faith's measure and turned to Wolfe. "Show me."

Wolfe opened the entrance to the secret room and the police officers followed him inside, their big flashlights beaming. Faith had no desire to take another look at her unfortunate predecessor.

Within a couple of minutes, the officers emerged, Garris speaking into his shoulder microphone as he walked to the open French door. "Get the coroner over here and call in Tobin and Rooney. Tell them to bring the crime scene kit."

The chief's words jolted Faith. "Was it foul play?" she asked Officer Laddy.

The young officer's handsome face had a decidedly green cast. "I really can't say, Miss Newberry. That's up to the coroner."

"But the crime—" Before she could finish her sentence, he shook his head and turned away, heading to join Garris on the terrace.

Wolfe came to stand beside Faith. "You'd better stick around." His voice was low. "They'll have questions for you." His mouth twisted in a semblance of a smile. "And me."

Someone pounded on the thick wood of the library door, startling Faith. "Who could that be?"

The retreat owner's smile was ironic. "Three guesses." After the knocking continued, he said, "I guess I'd better answer before she breaks down the door."

"What took you so long?" Marlene Russell vibrated with anger. She put her hands on her hips. "And why are the police here? You wouldn't say."

"Come in, Marlene, and shut the door behind you." Wolfe's tone was soothing. "You don't want to cause a panic, do you?"

"A panic?" Marlene glanced both ways, then darted into the library. Wolfe shut the door behind her and locked it again. "Faith. I might have known. Is something wrong? Is that why the police are here?"

"You could say that, Marlene," Faith said. She gestured toward the wall alcove. "We just, ah . . ."

"Found Doris Lincoln's body," Wolfe finished crisply. "So of course I phoned the chief right away."

Marlene was literally rocked on her heels by the news. Shock registered as her green eyes widened. Then she rallied. "Well, as assistant manager, I should have been informed immediately that a former employee was found dead."

Wolfe's shrug was dismissive. "I thought you would be busy with dinner. I am the GM and owner after all. Surely I provide adequate coverage of the situation."

Marlene merely grunted as she moved toward the opening, craning her neck to peer into the dark. "What happened? Could you tell?"

"You don't want to go in there, Marlene. And no, we aren't sure how Doris died. That's up to the coroner and the crime scene techs."

At his words, Marlene collapsed on the settee beside Faith. "Crime scene techs? So it was foul play?" She thrust both hands into her hair, disarranging her neat chignon. "If this gets out, the manor's reputation will be ruined—ruined, I tell you."

Wolfe gritted his teeth. "Let me worry about that."

Poor Wolfe. The situation was bad enough without Marlene spouting predictions of disaster. With relief, Faith spotted additional official vehicles pulling into the parking lot. The sooner law enforcement finished their unpleasant but necessary task, the sooner the retreat could go back to business as usual.

Unless Doris had been murdered. In that case, the trouble was only beginning.

The crime scene officers were first to enter, lugging in standing lights and equipment boxes, followed by Garris and Laddy. After donning gloves and booties, the techs disappeared into the alcove with their stuff.

Next to appear was a short, balding man with glasses and a forward-leaning gait, carrying a medical bag. Faith guessed he was the coroner. "Where is the body?" he asked the chief, glancing over at Faith and Marlene.

Not here, Faith wanted to answer but she refrained.

"Follow me, Dr. Greco," Garris said, preceding him to the opening.

"Inside the wall?" Dr. Greco shook his head. "That's a new one on me."

After what seemed an interminable time but was actually ten minutes according to the mantel clock, the chief reemerged into the library. "When was the last time any of you saw Doris Lincoln?" he asked. Officer Laddy pulled out his phone, ready to take notes.

"A few weeks ago," Wolfe said. "I was out of town on business until ten days ago. When I came back, I was told she had quit."

"Can you confirm that, Wolfe?" Garris asked.

"Of course. You can check with my assistant. She makes all my travel arrangements."

"Give Laddy her contact information, okay? Ms. Russell, when did you last see Ms. Lincoln?"

Marlene began to jiggle her knees. "The Saturday of Labor Day weekend." Her voice rose to a shrill pitch. "The day she quit without notice."

Garris nodded as if that confirmed something. "I'll need a list of everyone who was on site that day. Staff, guests, vendors, everyone."

The manager blanched. "I hope you don't plan on questioning our guests. They'll never come back. They'll probably post bad reviews on the Internet too."

The chief frowned. "Look, Ms. Russell, this isn't pleasant for anyone. But when it's a murder investigation, people need to cooperate. I'm sure your guests will understand."

Marlene gasped. "Murder? You think Doris was murdered?" She cast a fearful glance at the open alcove. "I thought she got trapped in there or something."

That's what Faith had initially thought. That scenario was bad enough, but the confirmation of foul play sent a chill up her spine. Who had killed Doris Lincoln—and why?

Judging by the skeptical expression on Jan Rooney's pretty face, the police officer thought she had found a worthy suspect in Faith. "So, Miss Newberry, you claim you never met Ms. Lincoln?"

Faith, Officer Rooney, and Officer Mick Tobin were in the den located off the library, the spot Garris had designated for interviews.

"That's right, Officer," Faith said for the third time. "The only time I might have crossed paths with her is when we both applied for the job six months ago. But I didn't see any of the other candidates that day."

"You must have been surprised when they called you and said there was a vacancy," Tobin said. In contrast to Officer Rooney's aloof demeanor, the blond, short, slightly paunchy Tobin was warm and friendly.

"I was. Very surprised." Faith's impulse was to say more, to blurt how thrilled she had been to get the job. But whatever she said could and would be used against her, right?

Rooney switched gears, pretending to study her notes. "Your aunt lives in Lighthouse Bay, you said."

"She does. Eileen Piper. She's the librarian at the Candle House Library."

"Like aunt, like niece. That's cool." Tobin grinned as if he'd never heard something so delightful. He leaned his chair back on two legs, but when the antique creaked, he hastily thumped back down.

"Did you ever visit her?" Rooney's dark almond-shaped eyes never left Faith's face.

Faith felt heat surge up her neck. "Of course. Not often, but I did." Her heart began to pound when she realized what was next. Could Rooney sense the fear filling her core like cold black water?

"When was the last time, do you recall?" Rooney's frosty tone told her she would verify everything Faith said.

Faith sucked in air, hoping it would help her calm down. She had to tell the truth. "Labor Day weekend. I was with my aunt the whole time. You can ask her."

Rooney and Tobin exchanged glances. "Don't leave town, Miss Newberry," Rooney said. "We may want to talk to you again."

4

Faith exited the den, every molecule in her body urging escape. She wanted nothing more than to gather her cat and leave. Where should she go? The cottage no longer seemed a cozy refuge. Maybe she should go to Eileen's house. Maybe she should quit her job. Maybe—

"Whoa, Faith. What's the hurry?" Wolfe reached out a hand to detain her.

Faith jerked a thumb at the den, where the two officers were now grilling their next victim, Brooke. "According to them, I'm a murder suspect, so quite frankly I want to get out of here." She glanced around, not seeing her cat. "Where's Watson?" She groaned silently. She hoped he wouldn't pull another one of his disappearing acts. *Look what happened the last time.* Were there more dead bodies lurking in the walls of Castleton Manor? Hysterical laughter bubbled up in her chest, pressing for release.

"Faith." Wolfe's voice was gentle. "We're all suspects right now. They're just doing their job." He shook her shoulder gently. "Look at me."

She forced herself to meet his eyes. Despite her distress she saw the kindness in his brilliant blue gaze. Then a terrible thought intruded. *How well do I know this man?* Not at all, actually, and he was a Jaxon, sworn enemy of the Newberrys for generations. Maybe he was guilty and she would be his convenient scapegoat. After all, how many people knew about the secret room?

Faith pulled her arm away from his grasp, hoping he hadn't read her unruly thoughts. "I'm sorry. It's been a long day—a very long day—and I need to go home." Wherever that was.

Confidence in her future at the retreat was definitely shaken.

Wolfe stepped out of her way. "I understand. Get some sleep, and we'll talk in the morning." He pointed to the dark space under the desk. "I think Watson is hiding under there."

Faith had to crouch on the floor to coax him out, aware all the while of the bustle of police going back and forth behind her back. She gathered him in her arms, picked up her tote, and headed for the French doors, the quickest way out of the building. Maybe she could shed a little more DNA on the way out for them to use in their case against her.

A crowd of retreat guests were milling around on the terrace outside the library, herded to one side so as not to interfere with the police. So the word about Doris was out, and no doubt this true-crime event was much more compelling than after-dinner speeches.

"What happened, Faith?" a woman's voice called. Faith saw one of the guests who had attended her lecture waving an arm at her. *Great.*

"Is it true you found her body?" another shouted out.

"I really can't comment," she said. Faith ducked her head and picked up her pace. Straight ahead, a dog whined, and she recognized Molly, standing next to her owner, Benedict Sinclaire. Fortunately Benedict had her leashed this time. Faith clutched a squirming Watson tighter. "Do not jump down."

"Behind you. Move it, please." A man's urgent voice warned.

Faith whirled around to see two men pushing a gurney out of the library, a black bag resting on top. A black bag containing the remains of the unfortunate Doris Lincoln. She jumped aside, her ankle twisting on the flagstones as her heel came down.

"Steady there." Benedict grabbed her arm.

"Sorry," Faith said. "I seem to be making a habit of falling over."

They moved back toward the edge of the terrace, well out of

the way as the gurney rumbled toward the coroner's van. Molly gave a whining yip, but her interest wasn't in Watson this time. Lurching forward against her leash, she strained to reach the gurney, howling.

Benedict tugged the dog back. "No, Molly." The dog returned to his side but continued to cry and whine until the gurney was loaded and the van drove off. The dog's reaction was extreme, as if Molly had known Doris quite well. If that was the case, it meant Benedict probably did too. How close had they been?

Back at the cottage, Faith ushered Watson inside and closed and locked the door. She kicked off her shoes and headed for the bedroom, eager to change into comfy jammies. After washing up and putting the kettle on the stove, she grabbed her cell phone. She needed help and support and she needed it now.

Eileen's knock came mere minutes later, while Faith was filling the teapot with steaming water. She set the kettle down and rushed to answer the door.

"Thanks for coming over," Faith said, standing back so her aunt could step inside. She glanced both ways, then closed and locked the door again.

"What's this all about, Faith?" Eileen shrugged out of her tweed coat and hung it on the hall tree. "I saw a cruiser and an ambulance leaving the manor when I drove in."

"Take a seat and I'll tell you all about it." Faith led the way to the living room, where she added a log to the fire. She reached for the poker before remembering that there wasn't one. She used the shovel again instead. "Do you want tea?"

"Sure. That sounds nice. It's getting chilly out there." Eileen settled back on the sofa without asking any more questions. Watson jumped up beside her and curled into a ball.

Faith brought the tray in from the kitchen and poured them each a cup. "I have terrible news, Aunt Eileen." She bit her lip, finding it hard to talk without crying. But she had to explain. Her aunt was probably dying inside with concern and anxiety. All Faith had said on the phone was that she had an emergency.

She took a deep breath. "Doris Lincoln is dead and I'm afraid they think I killed her." Her words were one fast and furious rush.

Eileen jolted back in her seat, her tea slopping toward the rim of the cup. "What?" She steadied her cup. "Can you say that again, please?"

Faith explained how Watson had gotten caught behind the library wall and when she and Wolfe Jaxon released him, they discovered Doris.

"Oh my. So she's been there since Labor Day weekend? And everyone thought she was off having a great time on her cruise." Eileen shook her head. "How sad."

"The worst part is that they think she was murdered. I'm not quite sure how since they didn't share that, but like I said, they think it was me."

Eileen set her cup on the side table. "You? You never met the woman. Why do they believe such a ridiculous thing?"

Faith gestured around the pleasant room. "For this. For the job. At least that's what the police officers implied." Her stomach gave a lurch. "And the worst thing is, I was here that weekend. So I don't have an alibi."

"Of course you do. You were with me the entire weekend."

"No I wasn't." Faith set down her cup and put both hands over her face. "Remember? You had to go take care of Madison on Sunday while Eric and Claire took Benjamin to the ER for his broken arm." Eric was Eileen's son and he and his wife, Claire, had two children. They lived in Provincetown, Rhode Island.

"I was gone only a few hours. You said you'd stay home and wait for me to get back."

"That's what I did." Faith remembered it well. "It was pouring out so I curled up with a book."

"So what's the problem? You weren't anywhere near this place."

"But don't you get it? If she died around that time, they won't believe me. According to Brooke, the manor was deserted that weekend. So theoretically I could have left your house, come here, and killed her."

Eileen jumped up from the sofa and gave Faith a hug. "There is no reason to panic. You don't know what the evidence will show. I'm sure the questioning was routine." She patted Faith's back and released her.

Faith wasn't sure of that at all, but she decided to accept her aunt's reasoning for the moment. "All right. I'll try not to climb the walls while I wait." She gave a shaky laugh. "Good thing Dad is out of the country or he'd be all over this."

Faith's father, Martin Newberry, was a retired police sergeant. He and her mother, Barbara, were on a once-in-a-lifetime cruise in the Mediterranean, visiting Italy and Greece. She'd been a little worried about them being out of cell phone reach, but now she was thankful. There was no way she was going to ruin their vacation by filling them in some other way, either.

"You're right about that. Martin was a very good detective." Eileen plopped down on the sofa.

Faith took a deep breath. Should she confide in Eileen about the forged book tonight? Why not? "I have something else to tell you."

"My goodness. What else could possibly have happened in just two days on the job?"

Faith stood and leaned against the mantel, poking the fire with the shovel. "The prized first-edition Sherlock Holmes in the Castleton Manor library is a fake."

Eileen gasped. "That edition of *A Study in Scarlet*? Are you sure?"

"Absolutely. It doesn't even feel or smell old. It's not only a copy, it's a bad copy." Faith shrugged. "Apparently no one ever takes it out of the case or they would have noticed."

"But who . . . and why?" Eileen furrowed her brow in puzzlement.

"For money, obviously. That book is worth a fortune." Faith sank onto the sofa beside her aunt. "I'd like to get a second opinion, of course, before I say anything to the Jaxons. Do you know anyone local who does appraisals?"

Eileen thought for a moment and then snapped her fingers. "Yes I do. Franklin Woodbury is an antiquarian book dealer here in town. And I believe he does some consulting and appraising. You can try him."

"I will." Faith studied the leaping flames, appreciating their warmth and comfort. "I wonder if Doris Lincoln knew about the book. Maybe that's why she was murdered."

"She didn't stay here very long so it's hard to say." Eileen glanced around the room. "Speaking of which, where are all her things?"

"Good point. There wasn't anything here but furniture when I moved in. Someone must have cleaned out the place."

"Before or after her death?" Eileen's tone was droll.

"That is the question." Faith stretched with a yawn. "Thanks for coming over, Aunt Eileen. I feel like maybe I'll sleep tonight after all."

Faith did sleep surprisingly well, assisted by the gentle patter of rain on the roof. Watson's warmth also helped, curled in a ball against her back. The ringing of her cell phone woke her.

"Faith?" The strident tones of the resort assistant manager greeted her. "Can you be here at eight? We're having a meeting with the conference leaders."

Faith pulled the phone away to peer at the time. Seven on the dot. That didn't give her much time to get ready. "I'll try to make it. I wasn't planning to come over until nine thirty, when I open."

Marlene snorted. "I'll expect to see you at eight." She disconnected.

"Reow?" With a growling mew, Watson butted her arm, one of his many signals for her to feed him.

Faith threw back the covers. "Yes, we're officially up for the day, Watson. Come on, I'll give you breakfast."

In a bit of a temper, Faith fed Watson, showered, and threw bread into the toaster for her own breakfast. Her hair was still slightly damp and her stockings were crooked when she left the house, but fortunately the rain had stopped and the bright sun promised a warm day.

Feeling slightly cheered, Faith turned to wave good-bye to Watson, watching from a window. "Be good, okay?" she called. "Don't dig up any more mysteries." He glared in response, then jumped off the sill with a twitch of his stubby tail.

Tamping down her guilt, Faith strode across the grounds toward the mansion, careful to stay on the path to avoid the wet grass. Today was a half day and she planned to go down to town after closing up. In addition to a couple of errands, a visit to Franklin Woodbury was on her list. She couldn't do anything about the police investigation of Doris's death, but she could look into the matter of the book forgery.

At the front desk, Faith was directed downstairs to Marlene's office. The lower level was the business area of the mansion, and Faith peeked curiously into the huge kitchen and bustling laundry as she went by. Marlene's office was at the end of a hallway lined with doors, their signs reading Head Chef, Head Housekeeper, Purchasing, and Accounting. Hers read Assistant Manager.

The door was ajar so Faith knocked and entered. A group of five people were seated around a conference table along one wall. In addition to Marlene and Wolfe, Faith recognized Benedict and the woman who wore a deerstalker's hat. The last person was an attractive older African-American woman with close-cropped hair.

"Hi, everyone," she said. "I'm Faith Newberry, the librarian."

"Glad you could make it, Faith." Marlene's tone asked, "What took you so long?" She waved a hand at the others. "Why don't you all introduce yourselves?" The deerstalker woman was Deb Cabot and the other woman was Sandra Baker. Along with Benedict, they were the conference leaders.

"Poor you," Deb said. "I heard you were the one who found the body." She reached down to pat her wolfhound on the head. "I can't believe Clancy didn't sniff it out."

"Actually, my cat found her," Faith said, settling in the empty chair between Benedict and Wolfe. "Somehow he got inside the secret chamber."

"Watson is quite the detective, isn't he?" Marlene's tone was disapproving.

"That's his name? Watson?" Deb laughed. "That's a hoot."

Fortunately, there was no mention of Faith's unpleasant interview with the police. Apparently they hadn't shared their suspicions about her involvement, and that realization made the knot in her belly relax slightly.

A young woman barged through the door carrying a tray with a coffee carafe, cups, and fixings. Thin, almost bony, with milk-white skin, she had pale blonde hair pulled back into a ponytail and light blue eyes. She wore the retreat's ubiquitous uniform of black pants and white blouse along with a name tag that read "Laura."

"It's about time," Marlene said. She pointed to a credenza. "Put it over there."

The waitress obeyed, setting the tray down with a rattle that sent a cup flying toward the floor. Somehow Benedict caught it, and he handed it back to her with a smile.

"Th-thanks," she stuttered. Wiping her hands on her pants, she asked, wide eyes fastened on Marlene, "Is there anything else?"

Marlene shook her head. "No, that's all." She turned her attention back to the group without even a thank-you. The waitress fled, banging the door shut behind her.

"Sorry for the interruption," Marlene said. "Help yourself to coffee."

"As I was saying," Sandra said, frowning at Deb, "I don't think we should cancel the conference." Surging to her feet, she went for the coffee tray.

"But continuing on isn't respectful to Ms. Lincoln." Benedict stroked Molly's floppy ears over and over. "We're acting like her death doesn't matter."

"Of course her death matters," Wolfe said. "In fact, why don't we have a moment of silence tonight at dinner?"

"That would be a nice touch," Deb said. "I never met the woman, but probably some of our guests have." She took a turn at the coffee setup.

Benedict ducked his head and once again Faith wondered about his connection to Doris. His emotion seemed excessive for a casual acquaintance.

"That's my point," Sandra said. "It is a tragedy, like any untimely demise, but most of the attendees haven't been here before. I'd hate to move the event back to Boston next year."

Sandra's subtle threat had a galvanizing effect on Marlene. "Don't do that. Look, we'll do all we can to make the rest of the conference go smoothly."

"Actually, I think they're eating it up." Deb waggled her brows. "They're a bloodthirsty bunch, you know."

"It's settled then." Sandra slapped the table and prepared to rise. "We're proceeding as scheduled." She glanced at the wall clock. "I'm heading up to breakfast. Anyone else?"

Faith managed to slip out in the general exodus, not sure exactly why her presence had been required. She'd worked for managers before who loved to throw their weight around because they could. Marlene appeared to be one of them.

She caught up to Benedict and Molly at the foot of the stairs, where he was scooping her up into his arms. "She must have trouble climbing stairs with those short legs."

"That's right, she does." Benedict trudged up the steps, the hem of his cape swinging.

Faith climbed beside him on the wide stairs, thinking about how to approach the topic. Finally she asked, "Did you know Ms. Lincoln well?"

Benedict was silent long enough for her to regret asking. "I was a writer in residence last month for my mystery novels," he said finally. "I met her then." They reached the top of the stairs and he set Molly down. "Come on, girl. I'll give you a sausage."

Faith watched as the pair proceeded down the corridor, Molly's nails clicking on the polished marble floor. Her intuition told her there was more to the story, much more. Why was Benedict downplaying his relationship with Doris when it was obvious he was upset? Did he know anything about her death?

A line was waiting in the gallery when Faith arrived at the library door. She inserted the key into the brass lock on the double doors. "Good morning, everyone. The library opens in an hour."

A rotund man with an unlit meerschaum pipe in his mouth straightened from a leaning pose against the wall. "Couldn't you let us in now? I've been waiting for half an hour already."

"So have I," a woman said. "I'm dying to check out the library."

"Someone already did," another person said in a loud stage whisper. Uneasy titters rippled through the group.

Deb was right—they were a bloodthirsty bunch. With a sigh, Faith pushed the tall door open. "Come on in."

The hectic pace kept up all morning, and Faith was thankful that she had only a half day. She didn't even get a break to use the restroom or find a cup of coffee. The upside was that many more people had availed themselves of the manor's excellent collection. Perhaps she should send a letter to the library association, telling them that a dead body was an infallible way to boost circulation.

5

Faith locked the door after the last straggler exited the manor's library. After a quick lunch at home, she planned to go down to Lighthouse Bay to see Franklin Woodbury. She had one more thing to do first. Keys jingling, she went to the glass case holding the supposed first edition of *A Study in Scarlet.*

Faith inserted the key in the lock and then paused, her conscience warring with her need to know the truth. She really should talk to Wolfe before taking one of his books off the premises. *But what if Wolfe was responsible for the forgery?* Her stomach wobbled at that thought. *And worse, what if he killed Doris to keep her quiet?* He had access to the rare books and the secret room. And as owner, he stood to benefit financially from selling the real book and replacing it with a fake.

She couldn't take the risk, plain and simple, of telling Wolfe—or anyone, except her aunt—what she was about to do. Using gloves, Faith wrapped the book carefully in a cloth and placed it inside a small cardboard box. This she stowed in the bottom of her tote.

As she turned to go, the empty space in the case shone like a beacon. Someone might come into the library and notice the book missing before she got back. She set the tote down and scanned the shelves, finding a book that resembled the edition in color and size. That should suffice unless someone studied the books in the case closely. With any luck, she'd replace it in an hour or two and no one would know the difference.

Despite the nature of her errand, Faith felt her spirits lift as she drove down to down to the charming village of Lighthouse Bay. The narrow, tree-lined, cobblestoned Main Street lined with clapboard and brick Colonial buildings was one of her favorite places. She adored the eclectic blend of historic ambiance with wonderful shopping and eating establishments.

After finding a parking space in a municipal lot near the Candle House Library, Faith grabbed her tote and set off on foot. The bookstore was a couple of blocks away, Eileen had said. The businesses were delightfully varied—*Butcher, baker, candlestick maker,* she recited to herself. After her errand, she would treat herself to something from Snickerdoodles, she decided.

Down an alley, she spotted a sign, Donatello Fine Leather Goods. *That must be where Doris bought her purse.* Faith took a slight detour to check out the window display. Handbags, boots, belts, and wallets filled the small space, each item a study in elegant simplicity. Even through the glass, the leather appeared soft and supple, burnished to a warm glow.

A middle-aged woman with dark curly hair appeared in the doorway. "Would you like to come in and look around?" she asked in an Italian accent. Attractive and petite, she wore a tan pantsuit with a pair of gorgeous shoe boots. Handmade, Faith guessed.

"I would love to, but I don't have time right now." Faith lifted her tote in explanation. "I'll be back though."

"Anytime, you are welcome."

Vowing to return soon to see if the Donatellos knew anything about Doris, Faith continued down Main Street. Woodbury Antiquarian Books announced a white sign with navy and gilt lettering. The store was brick, with bow windows flanking the navy blue and glass front door. With a jingle of bells, Faith stepped into the magical world of old books, the smell of dust and paper and leather like ambrosia to her nostrils.

Bookcases crammed with books filled most of the small space, and old red movie theater seats had been placed here and there for patrons. Along one wall was a counter stacked high with yet more books, backed by glass cabinets. *The rare books, no doubt.*

A thin, balding man in his midfifties shuffled out of the back room. Half-glasses were perched on his nose and he wore a wrongly buttoned cardigan, baggy wool trousers, and carpet slippers. "Help you?" he asked, peering over his glasses. He shuffled around behind the counter.

"I hope so." Faith set her tote in one of the empty spaces on the counter. "I need an expert opinion on a book."

His eyes sharpened. "I don't give opinions on anything but first editions."

"I understand." Faith reached into her tote.

"People bring in all kinds of junk, thinking I'm going to buy their pulp fiction and dime novels."

"That must be a problem," Faith said. It was on the tip of her tongue to mention she was an archival librarian, but she sensed Franklin Woodbury would be threatened rather than charmed by a collegial approach. Some people had to be the expert in the room; she'd seen his type before.

Faith laid the cloth-wrapped book on the counter and unveiled it for Franklin's inspection, watching him closely. Surprise flared in his pale gray eyes, then was replaced by calm indifference. He adjusted his glasses. "Where did you get that?"

"I'd rather not say. Client privilege." The book world was as rife as any other with secretive dealers, buyers, and sellers, so Faith knew she was on firm footing.

"*A Study in Scarlet* is Sir Arthur Conan Doyle's first work." Franklin pulled on cotton gloves and picked up the book. "Published in 1887, very few copies still exist." He burbled on about the book and its supposed provenance.

Faith knew all of that but she kept quiet. Inside she was seething with impatience. Couldn't he tell it was a fake? She had known the moment she touched it.

He opened the cover and perused the printed flyleaf, brow furrowed in concentration. Finally Faith couldn't take the suspense a moment longer. "There's something wrong with that book," she burst out.

His wooly gray brows rose. "What do you mean?"

"It's a fake. Can't you tell?" She stabbed a finger at the novel. "It doesn't feel right, it doesn't look right, and it doesn't even smell right."

"Smell right?" His brows wiggled like caterpillars on his pale face.

Faith bit back a laugh. Trust him to focus on something that made her look foolish. "It doesn't have that old-book smell."

He raised the book to his nose and inhaled, then shook his head. "Sorry, I'm just getting over a cold." He placed the book back on the cloth.

"Never mind." Faith sighed as she wrapped the book back up. "Do me a favor, all right? Ask around and see if anyone sold a real copy of that book."

"I can do that, I suppose." He pulled a piece of scrap paper from a stack and picked up a pen. "How do I reach you?"

"I'm Faith Newberry." Did she imagine the jerking of his hand when she said her name? She gave her cell number, then picked up her tote and turned to go.

The bells at the front door jingled as a man pushed his way inside. Faith immediately recognized Benedict Sinclaire. How could she not? Once again he wore his cape and deerstalker hat. As she pushed her way past with a hello and a quick pat on Molly's head, he tipped his hat, watching curiously as she exited.

Faith fumed as she strode up the sidewalk. Just her luck, running into someone from the retreat. What if Franklin Woodbury told Benedict about her errand? He'd recognize *A Study in Scarlet* from her presentation.

She halted, forcing a pair of women shoppers to veer around her. Should she call the bookseller and warn him to keep the matter confidential? Her hand hovered over the compartment where she stored her phone. But if she did that, it would send up a red flag for sure. Franklin would surely wonder why she was making that request after seeing Benedict at the shop.

Sighing, she realized she should proceed as though innocent. Cross any bridges when she got to them.

The Happy Tails Gourmet Bakery sign caught her eye and she detoured across the street. Maybe Midge was in. If not she could still buy Watson a treat. Maybe that would make up for his terrible introduction to Castleton Manor.

A buzzer sounded as she entered. "Faith!" Midge emerged from the back room. "I'm so glad you came by." She set Atticus on the counter. "What do you think?"

The Chihuahua sported a pair of sunglasses perched on his tiny, pointy nose. As Faith suppressed a laugh, Atticus reached up with one paw and attempted to push off the glasses.

"No, Atticus." Midge made an adjustment to the strap. "I had to get the goggle style so he couldn't take them off and eat them." She patted her pooch with both hands. "They protect his beautiful eyes from UV rays."

Now Faith had seen almost everything. People certainly went a bit nutty over their pets, and apparently that included veterinarians. Then she spotted the contents of the bakery case, which held delicious-looking trays of cookies, cupcakes, biscuits, and doughnuts. "These are for dogs? They look good enough to eat."

"You *can* eat them. All the ingredients are food grade." Midge plucked a small square resembling a brownie off a tray and fed it to Atticus.

"That's not chocolate, is it?" Faith had heard chocolate was bad for dogs—and cats.

"No, it's carob. But he loves it anyway." Midge regarded her dog fondly. "You're a good boy. Now go play." She lifted him off the counter. "I heard you had some excitement up at the manor."

Faith's chest tightened at the reminder. "We certainly did." She lowered her voice although she and Midge were alone in the store. "In fact, the police questioned me. I'm a suspect in Doris Lincoln's death."

"Well, slap my head and call me silly!" Midge's voice rose in outrage. "I've never heard anything so ridiculous. You didn't even know Doris, bless her heart."

"That's what I told them. But they didn't believe me." Faith grimaced. "That's one reason I popped in. I also wanted to buy Watson a treat. He had the unfortunate experience of finding Doris."

Midge gasped. "How awful. Poor baby." She gestured for Faith to follow her. "This is our cat section." As in the dog area, there were toys, outfits, and other necessary pet items along with treats.

"He'd like this toy." Faith picked out a little gray mouse that looked all too real.

"It has catnip inside." Midge pointed to jars and packets of treats. "We have kitty caviar in a can, crunchy chicken bites that clean their teeth too, and tuna-flavored macaroons. I call them tunaroons."

Watson loved tuna flavor. "I'll take those."

Midge grabbed a plastic bag and pulled a lid off one of the jars. "I'll give you a few to make sure he likes them. I know how fussy cats can be."

As Midge scooped out the treats, Faith asked, "You said at the book club meeting that you take care of Molly Sinclaire."

"I sure do." Midge sealed the bag, which had a ziplock top, and set it on a scale.

"Do you know if Benedict and Molly knew Doris?"

Midge shook her head. "I never saw them together or anything. Why do you ask? You think our Sherlock Holmes impersonator had something to do with the murder?"

"Not really. But Molly acted strange when the EMTs brought Doris out on the gurney. She was whining and moaning as if she knew her."

"Dogs do react when something bad happens to their humans." Midge wrote the price on the bag of treats. "Maybe they got acquainted when he was writer in residence a few weeks ago."

That was what Benedict had said. Disappointed she hadn't learned anything new, Faith pulled out her wallet. "What do I owe you?"

Snickerdoodles Bakery was across the street, and Faith decided to make one more detour, to buy a people treat. Despite her turkey sandwich at home, she was hungry. Or maybe it was the stress of murder and subterfuge. Those probably increased one's appetite.

In contrast to the other night, the bakery was packed with patrons. They filled the tables and stood in line to be waited on. As she joined the line, Faith glanced around, smiling, hoping to see a familiar face or make a new friend. To her surprise, most people turned their heads, refusing to meet her eyes.

How strange. She turned her gaze forward and studied the bakery case until it was her turn.

"Good afternoon, Faith. What can I get you?" Jane asked, her gloved hand poised to make a choice.

"Good afternoon to you too. I'll have a magic bar," Faith said. The chocolate chip, coconut, and pecan confection looked mouthwatering. Perfect comfort food. "And a couple of those lemon poppy seed muffins." She'd have them for breakfast.

"Good choices," Jane said, her standard remark no matter what people picked, Faith noticed. She slid the baked goods into a white paper bag and rang up the total.

As she handed Faith the slip, she leaned forward, and after glancing around, whispered, "A little warning, Faith. People are talking about the feud between the Newberrys and the Jaxons. They're saying Doris's death let you kill two birds with one stone."

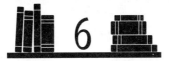

6

Faith grabbed the bag of baked goods and rushed out of the bakery, her ears burning in mortification. Was Jane serious? People actually thought that she had avenged an ancient wrong by killing Doris Lincoln?

Faith unlocked the car and threw her belongings inside, then backed out and peeled away a little faster than was prudent. But what was a speeding ticket on top of being a murder suspect? During the police interview, she had practically heard the jail cell doors clanging shut behind her. Thank goodness she had the support of her aunt and the rest of the book club. She certainly couldn't discuss her concerns with Marlene or Wolfe. She was half expecting to be fired already.

As she drove past the Candle House Library, she had an idea. She should search the local history section for information about Josiah Newberry's death. The story passed down through the family was sketchy at best, and all anyone really knew was that Josiah, business partner with Captain Angus Jaxon, died on Jaxon's ship. Subsequent financial difficulties were blamed on the Jaxons, but without more information it was impossible to know if Angus was really responsible for Newberry family troubles or whether he was nothing but a scapegoat.

She would start the project tonight, she decided, after doing some much-needed organizing at the cottage. But first she would stop at the library to return the purloined book resting in the bottom of her tote—before anyone noticed it was gone.

As Faith stepped inside the cottage a little later, Watson darted between her legs and ran outside, almost knocking her over. He always did that when he felt she had trapped him inside for too long. "Don't go too far," she called after him. "I've got treats."

The golden afternoon sunshine streaming into the cozy rooms comforted Faith and she felt herself relax. The magic bar from the bakery and a cup of coffee would give her an energy boost she sorely needed to tackle the rest of the unpacking.

She was pouring water into the coffeemaker when her phone rang, making her jump. Her heart pounding, she picked it up, expecting to see the police were calling. Instead it was a number she didn't recognize. "Hello?" she asked tentatively.

"Hey, Faith. This is Brooke. You know, from the book group. And the retreat, of course, where we both work." Her laughter pealed out.

Faith's shoulders slumped in relief. "Hi, Brooke. How are you?"

"I'm okay." Brooke's sigh said volumes, a whole saga about her trials and tribulations. "But I'm not calling to talk about me. I want to bring you dinner. That is, if you're free."

Faith was touched by the other woman's consideration. "How nice. I'm going over to the library later, but I don't have dinner plans." She glanced at her almost-empty shelves. "In fact, I wasn't sure what I was going to make tonight."

"All right then. I'll be there at five thirty."

The cat finished licking his dish, then flicked his tongue to get the last taste of clam chowder off his whiskers. Living by the ocean certainly had its perks.

His human was laughing, a sound that made a purr bubble up inside him. He rubbed against her legs, then those of her guest, whose trousers smelled delightfully of seafood.

Something under the radiator caught the flickering candlelight. What could that be? Intrigued, he trotted over and thrust his paw underneath. The object rolled out easily and scooted across the floor. What fun! He ran after the shiny bauble and began to bat it back and forth, exactly as those humans did with their hockey sticks.

After an especially powerful slap shot, the object skated right under his human's foot. Score!

Faith felt something hard hit the ball of her sock-clad foot. "What was that?" She bent down and retrieved the item. Her heart gave a thump of excitement. It was a cuff link in the shape of Sherlock Holmes's distinctive profile. She immediately thought of Benedict Sinclaire. Had he left it here?

"Look what Watson found." Faith handed the cuff link to Brooke. "Do you recognize it?"

Brooke held the cuff link between her thumb and forefinger. "I don't." Her eyes widened. "Are you thinking it belongs to someone at the Sherlock Holmes retreat?"

"Possibly. But Wolfe is the only man from Castleton who has been in here since I moved in." She thought about that. If Wolfe lost a cuff link while visiting, surely he would have said something. It must have been here since Doris's residency.

Brooke set the cuff link on the tablecloth. "Maybe it's a clue. Maybe Doris's killer left it." With a shiver, she glanced around. "I can't believe I actually said that out loud."

"I know. It's one thing to read about murders, but quite another to experience them personally . . ." *And to be suspected of committing one.* Faith's lips tightened at the thought. Should she confide in Brooke? With a sigh, she decided she had to. She needed all the help she could get in finding the real culprit. "You know I'm a prime suspect."

Brooke, busy buttering one of the flaky biscuits she had baked, dropped her knife with a clatter. "What? That's crazy. You didn't even know Doris."

"That's right, I didn't. But because of me getting her job and the feud between the Newberrys and the Jaxons, everyone has me tried, convicted, and condemned." Bitter anguish filled Faith's heart. This was not the way she imagined her new start in life going, not in a million years.

"Well, I certainly don't think you did it." Brooke's eyes glowed with fervor. "It's ridiculous. We have to find out who did, that's all."

Faith's heart warmed at this support. "Brooke, I'm certainly glad to have you on my team." An inspiration struck. "I'm going to approach this situation like a research project. I've done tons of those in my career."

"You mean with index cards and notes?"

"Partially. First I frame the question, then I gather information, trying to keep an open mind and be objective. I don't jump to conclusions. Then I see where the evidence leads." Faith shrugged. "The challenge is going to be keeping my emotions out of it. It's not fun being a suspect."

"I know what you mean." Brooke shuddered. "I didn't like being questioned, either. I almost felt like confessing, they made me feel so guilty."

"Exactly." Faith got up and retrieved a lined pad and pen. "Let's start now. When was the last time you saw Doris?"

Brooke propped her chin on her hand. "Hmm. Let me think. I know she was at Saturday breakfast. I remember giving her a second helping of pancakes when I was serving."

"What time was that?" Faith reached out and stroked Watson,

who had jumped up to sit in the empty chair beside her. He stared at Brooke, twitching his tail as if he were also listening.

"Let's see. It was around eight thirty." Brooke thought for a moment. "Yes, I'm pretty sure."

Faith wrote that down, as the starting point for a timeline. "Who was she eating with, do you remember?"

Brooke shook her head. "No, I'm sorry. The dining room was pretty crowded, and I was focused on giving out food." Then a startled expression passed over her face.

"What is it? Did you remember something?"

"Yes, but I'm not sure it means anything." She shrugged. "How could it?"

"Tell me anyway. You never know which detail might lead to something important." That was often the case in academic research anyway.

"After Doris left the table, she collided with one of the waitresses. Laura. You probably don't know her."

Faith remembered the young woman who had served them in Marlene's office. "I might. Is she blonde and pretty? Quite tall and thin?"

"Yes, that's her. She's nice but a total klutz."

That tallied with Faith's experience. "So I noticed."

"Anyway, Doris had an absolute fit, especially because Laura spilled coffee on her suit. She chewed the poor girl out and made her cry."

"Gosh, that's awful." Faith imagined the scene, the embarrassment of being scolded in front of a full dining room.

"It was. Laura ran into the kitchen and Doris stormed off." Brooke thought for a moment. "You don't think—"

"That Laura killed Doris? It's hard to imagine, she seems so gentle and sweet." Faith sighed. "But I'll record the incident. We need to keep an open mind, right?" She made a note. "What happened after breakfast? Did you see Doris again?"

"I'm afraid not. After we cleaned up, the kitchen staff left around noon. The guests were all gone by then since the retreat was closed Sunday and Monday." She grinned. "We don't get many free weekends, and we all took off like we had been shot out of a cannon."

Faith tapped her pen on the table. The killer certainly had found a perfect opportunity to commit the crime since the retreat was rarely closed. "Hmm. I think we need to find out if anyone else saw Doris that morning. Maybe they noticed if she was sitting with a guest or arguing with someone. Besides Laura."

Brooke snapped her fingers. "Good idea. I'll ask the other staff. Casually, of course. They're certainly gossiping about it already." At Faith's downturned mouth, she added, "Don't worry. If they mention you, I'll tell them you're innocent."

"I appreciate that." Faith thought over what Brooke had shared. "How was Doris with the rest of the staff?"

Brooke sighed. "I know we have to discuss this, but I feel terrible. Don't speak ill of the dead and all that."

"Normally I would agree with you. But someone hated Doris enough to kill her. And somehow I doubt it was a random event committed by a stranger."

"That's true. She wouldn't have ended up in the secret room if that were the case." Brooke grabbed another biscuit. "The thing is, Doris wasn't here very long. And she was kind of odd. She never really fit in, not like you."

"What do you mean?" Faith was flattered by Brooke's praise.

"Well, with me she was aloof. She did this snooty librarian thing where she looked over her glasses at me." Brooke laughed. "She made me feel like I must have mishandled a book or something."

"I've known librarians like that. Anything else?"

"She was always getting in tiffs with people. I heard her arguing with Marlene almost every day. She didn't like the way the library was set up or how they scheduled the hours. And the records were a mess, according to her."

Those seemed like reasonable concerns, but apparently Doris wasn't exactly tactful in handling people. A thought galvanized her: *Maybe Doris had discovered the theft and bluntly questioned the wrong person.* Faith wanted to confide in Brooke about the forged book but decided to wait until she figured out how to handle the situation.

"How about Wolfe?" Faith tried to keep her tone casual. He was the logical person for Doris to approach.

"She was always after him too. I guess when she didn't get her way with Marlene, she'd go over her head to Wolfe."

"Wow. That's not very tactful." Faith shook her head.

"I know. If she hadn't died, they might have let her go, I think." Brooke grinned. "They should have hired you in the first place."

"Oh, how I wish they had!" Perhaps Doris would still be alive. That is, if her death did have something to do with someone at Castleton Manor.

After Brooke left—fortunately, leaving the yummy chowder leftovers behind—Faith drove down to the Candle House Library. Her decision to do her own investigation had given her new energy. She wasn't going to sit idle and let the police build a case against her.

Only a couple of cars were in the parking lot, and after locking her car, Faith hurried toward the building. A gust of wind rattled the dying leaves on a maple outside the door, making her shiver and draw her collar up around her ears. Winter was coming, that was certain.

Inside, Eileen was behind the front desk. She set down the volume she was browsing. "Faith. What brings you down here tonight?"

Faith unbuttoned her coat, grateful for the warm gusts of heat blowing from the vents. "I'd like to research the story of Josiah Newberry and Angus Jaxon." She grimaced. "Some people are saying it's one of the reasons I murdered Doris Lincoln."

Eileen's mouth dropped open. "What people? That's ridiculous."

"I think so too. Jane from the bakery gave me a friendly warning about it." Faith hung her coat on a hook. "So I'm going to find out what really happened on that boat in eighteen-whatever."

"June 1825," Eileen said. "We've got the old local papers on microfilm if you want to look at them. I'd try the *Lighthouse Bay Observer.*"

"I will. I'll also look for anything else from that period." Faith picked up her tote.

"There are also town records in the archives." Eileen came around the desk, gesturing for Faith to follow. "Upstairs."

As they walked through the back hallway to the stairs, Faith noticed a staff kitchen followed by a small room filled with long tables holding stacks of books. "What's going on in there?"

Eileen glanced over. "Those are the books for our annual sale. We have volunteers organizing them by topic and value." She smiled at Faith. "Quite a few were donated by Castleton Manor. So if you come across anything else you don't want, feel free to bring them down. Or I can send someone to get them."

That was good to know. Apparently the library at Castleton Manor, like many public libraries, did periodic cleanups to get rid of books that were duplicates, donations, or no longer of interest. "I'll do that," Faith said. Personally she hated taking books out of a collection, feeling a pang of sadness at releasing them as if they were unwanted kittens, but at least here the proceeds were going to a worthy cause. And hopefully the books all found a good home.

The second story of the old factory building was a warren of rooms, no doubt used for storage or offices. Eileen unlocked a door and ushered Faith inside. She flicked a switch, revealing bookcases full of leather-bound volumes and storage units, plus a worktable holding a computer and a microfilm reader. "It's not fancy, but you'll find what you need in here."

Faith inhaled the odor of old paper and ink, a familiar sense of excitement humming in her veins. She recognized it as the thrill of the hunt, something only other research nerds would understand. Who knew what treasures she would discover?

Eileen went to the computer and turned it on. "The card catalog is on here so you can figure out what you want to look at and then find it on the shelves." She pulled open a file cabinet drawer. "The newspaper microfilm is in here, arranged by journal and date. The 1825 issues are in this drawer, since they're among the earliest."

"Thanks for all your help." Faith set her tote down and pulled out the chair at the worktable. "This is great."

Her aunt patted Faith's shoulder. "You're a woman after my own heart. I can't wait to find out what you discover." She moved toward the door. "I'd better get back downstairs. Let me know if you need anything."

"I will." The door shut softly behind Eileen, and Faith turned her attention to the computerized catalog of the historical archives. In addition to archives of newspapers, the room held a variety of books and records related to the town and region. She hadn't read much about Lighthouse Bay's past, so the first thing she did was check for local histories. There were several volumes, the first written in the early 1800s, the next one in the late 1800s, and one a recent three-hundred-year retrospective.

She quickly found those on a shelf and carried them back to the table. Fortunately the later two were indexed, the first being only an account of colorful tales from different parts of Cape Cod titled *An Early History of Lighthouse Bay and Cape Cod*. Definitely something to read later, when she had more time.

The Newberrys and the Jaxons were listed as among the first settlers to arrive in Lighthouse Bay in the 1600s. She skimmed ahead to the 1800s, when Angus Jaxon rose to prominence as a sea captain transporting American goods to England. Her ancestor, Josiah Newberry, was described as a businessman with many interests, including investing in cargo with Angus.

At the end of that section was a telling sentence, "The Newberry fortunes suffered a sharp reversal when Josiah Newberry died at sea in 1825." Faith leafed ahead and found no further reference to Josiah.

Footsteps sounded outside the room, thudding on the wooden floor of the hall. They approached, then stopped. Faith waited for someone to step into the room, but no one did. Was it Eileen, hesitant to disturb her?

"Aunt Eileen? Is that you?"

No answer. After a long moment, Faith got up and went to the doorway. The dimly lit hall was deserted. A couple of doors stood open but all the rooms were dark.

How strange. Faith shrugged and went back to her work. After a glance at her watch and seeing she only had half an hour until closing time, she decided to load up the microfilm from June 1825 to see if the local newspaper reported Josiah's death.

She went to the file cabinet and pulled out the drawer, which voiced a screech as it opened. She looked through the marked boxes for the right year.

What was that? Her spine stiffened at the odd sound and she cocked her head, listening. Nothing. Now she was imagining things.

Faith loaded up the film in the reader and set it to whirring, steeling herself against the odor and the motion, which tended to make her nauseated. The newspapers were weekly, which meant that once she accessed 1825, there were only twenty or so issues to scan through to find June.

Early newspapers were much more dense, mostly text with very few illustrations and smaller headlines. She scoured June, finding nothing. Finally, in the August 3, 1825, issue, she found an article. "Town mourns loss of prominent citizen at sea." Apparently the *Honoria* didn't dock until August, although the incident happened in June, when Josiah became ill and died when the ship was off the coast of England. It took an additional six weeks for the ship to reach Massachusetts.

So Josiah died of an illness. Not uncommon, surely. She sat and stared at the article, pondering what might have happened—or what people believed. Had her ancestors thought Angus killed Josiah and covered up the murder by claiming it was illness that took his life? Or if not, what else happened to cause the rift?

A slight breath of air touched the back of her neck, making her hair stand on end. Why did she suddenly feel as if eyes were watching her? The intensity of the sensation between her shoulder blades was so great that she didn't dare to turn her head. Feeling pinned in place, chills ran along her shoulders and arms and a bead of sweat trickled down her back.

Finally, gathering all her courage, she whirled around in her chair. Once again, no one was there.

7

Totally unnerved, Faith turned off the microfilm reader and removed the roll, her fingers shaking. She'd have to come back another day, preferably in the daylight when other people were around. Ever the conscientious professional, she replaced the history books and finished tidying up before gathering her things and fleeing.

As she clattered down the back stairs, she heard the distinct sound of a door slamming shut. Was that a back door? She certainly couldn't hear the front door from here.

Faith peeked around the corner into the kitchen, where an exit sign hung. The room was dark, and the door, with its glass pane and ruffled curtain, stood innocently silent. She shook her head. Maybe a patron went out that way for some reason.

In the main room, Eileen looked up from her computer at her entrance. "There you are. I was just coming to get you. It's closing time."

"I remembered." Faith hesitated. "Did you see anyone go out the back way?"

Her aunt shook her head. "No. I've been alone for the past half hour. Why do you ask?" She turned off her computer and began to pick up her belongings and stow them in her bag.

"I thought I heard someone." Faith attempted a laugh. "I guess I got spooked by this creaky old building."

Eileen frowned but she didn't comment. "Any luck with your research?" She came around the desk, Faith following along as she switched off lights and turned down the heat.

"Some. I did find a story about Josiah's death. Next I want to dig into the family background and find out why they were so angry with Angus Jaxon. Right now his death doesn't appear suspicious."

Eileen let Faith out and then shut the heavy front door behind them and inserted the key. "Feuds often grow from the smallest things. Then after a while no one remembers how they even got started."

"That's probably true with this one too. I hope so." If she discovered the feud was imaginary or trumped up, then she would make sure everyone in town gossiping about the story knew the truth.

The duo walked down the wide granite steps, parting with calls of "Good night!" as they headed for their cars. As Faith went around the corner of the building, she saw a tall figure standing there, near the wall.

She jumped, her heart pounding. Then she heard a familiar squeak and thump. Someone was putting books in the after-hours drop.

Laughing at herself, she continued along the sidewalk, and as she drew closer, she saw it was Wolfe Jaxon. "Hi, Wolfe. Fancy meeting you here." She cleared her throat to cover her shaking voice.

"Faith. Can't get enough of libraries, hmm?" He smiled to let her know he was joking.

"I could say the same for you. Are you stepping out on the Castleton Manor library?"

He chuckled, running a hand through his hair. He wore a wool overcoat but no hat. "I'm returning books for my mother. We have a great collection, but of course we don't buy every single mystery published."

"Oh, she's a mystery fan? My aunt is too, obviously."

Eileen had created a well-stocked section in the Candle House Library called "Mystery Loves Company." Faith jingled her keys. "Here's my car. I guess I'll say good night."

Wolfe gave a wave as he strode away. "Good night, Faith. See you tomorrow." He disappeared into the dark and a moment later Faith heard the distinctive purr of his BMW sedan.

She hastily unlocked the car and jumped in, throwing her tote into the passenger seat. Then she locked the doors. Only by sheer force of will had she maintained what she hoped was a semblance of composure.

Someone had been up on the second floor. She had definitely heard footsteps. And while one might imagine all kinds of creepy things, footsteps were hard to explain away. Had Wolfe been lurking in the library, spying on her?

The next morning, Faith headed over to the manor early. She planned to have breakfast and browse the vendors in the Great Hall Gallery before opening the library.

Tables lined both sides and the middle of the long, high-ceilinged room, which was thronged with guests and echoing with chatter and laughter. Faith enjoyed seeing the amusing variety of merchandise for sale. If she felt so inclined, she could buy a Sherlock Holmes teddy bear, wall clock, or Christmas tree ornament. She did succumb to a mug printed with the slogan The Game's Afoot, but she successfully resisted Sherlock dolls, jewelry, and apparel. Someone could furnish an entire house with Sherlock stuff, she realized with amusement.

Franklin Woodbury, the book dealer, was hosting a booth displaying various Sherlock editions. He was deep in conversation with Deb, the deerstalker-clad attendee and conference leader, her wolfhound sitting patiently at her side. As Faith approached, Franklin glanced up and acknowledged her with a nod, then continued his discussion, lowering his voice.

Faith hovered to one side, waiting, checking over the books for sale. It wasn't any of her business what they were talking about, but she had to admit she was curious, especially when she overheard Deb say, "I'd hate to go elsewhere, Franklin. So do your best." She strode away, heels clacking on the polished floor, tugging on her dog's leash so he followed.

Franklin turned and began to straighten already perfectly aligned books on the table. The back of his neck was red, Faith noticed.

"Customers can be difficult, can't they?" Faith smiled. "So can my library patrons. At my old job, they were always hounding me about the speed of interlibrary loans."

Franklin muttered something indistinct, then, "How can I help you, Miss Newberry?"

"I was wondering if you had any luck yet. Finding any recent sales of *Scarlet,* that is."

The bookseller glanced up sharply. "I'm afraid I haven't. It's far too soon for answers to come back." He waved a hand. "Everyone is so busy these days." His tone implied that he was also, and she was pressuring him.

Faith felt suitably chastened. She straightened her shoulders into what she hoped was a dignified pose. "Please keep me posted." She glanced at her watch. "Oops. Got to run. Have a good day." She strode away, mimicking a woman on a mission rather than someone fleeing.

With a sigh, she achieved the quiet sanctuary of the library and set about getting ready for the day. On the precise dot of nine, she unlocked the door and switched the sign to Open.

The first person through the door wasn't a patron. It was Laura, the clumsy maid. She waved a feather duster. "I'm here to clean."

Faith gestured at the towering shelves. "Be my guest. Although I'd be happy to help."

"No problem, I like working in here." Laura began to dust the shelves near the desk where Faith was seated. "Is it fun being a librarian?"

"It is, most days." Faith laughed. Actually, she loved her chosen career. Since the first time she entered a library as a child, she had been enchanted by a world full of stories, information, and knowledge about every topic under the sun. To work daily with books was a dream come true. Sharing that passion was her mission in life.

Laura paused the brisk movement of her duster. "I always wanted to work in a library. I love books and it would sure beat being a maid." Faith regarded her with sympathy. "It's still possible, you know. It does require a college degree . . ."

The young woman's face was eager. "I've got some credits already. Maybe I should go back—" In her excitement she stepped backward, bumping into a table and knocking over a stack of books. "Oops! I'm sorry." She whirled around, dropped the duster, and bent to pick up the hardcovers and paperbacks.

Biting back a smile, Faith jumped up to help her. The young woman was amazingly clumsy. "No problem. These really should have been put away." Someone had obviously been in the library after hours. She always made sure all the books were filed before closing for the day. Who could it have been? As far as she knew, only Marlene and Wolfe had keys.

Laura's voice distracted Faith from her thoughts. "You're much nicer than that other librarian. She was always yelling at me about something or another." She pressed her lips together. "She even tried to get me fired."

Faith could understand Doris's probable frustration with the maid, but in her eyes, the young woman's endearing qualities made up for her lack of grace. Doris's reaction seemed extreme. Before she could probe further, the doorknob rattled and Marlene swept in, key ring jingling.

"There you are," the manager said to Laura. "You're needed in the Agatha Christie suite. A sick dog vomited on the carpet." Marlene's nose wrinkled. "Clean it quick before the rug is stained permanently."

"Right away, Ms. Russell." Laura lurched forward, this time tripping over an ottoman in her haste to obey her boss. To Faith's relief, she regained her balance before landing face-first on the floor.

"Which dog is it?" Faith asked, curious.

Marlene sniffed. "That little mutt Molly. She's always getting sick from one thing or another. We had to call in the vet again. She's up there now." She cast a critical eye around the library, then swept out again.

Laura trotted toward the door. "I'd better get up there."

Faith made a snap decision. "Wait a minute. I'll come with you." She could see how Molly was doing and say hello to Midge. She turned the sign to Closed and locked the door again. What good was being in charge if one couldn't take an unscheduled break now and then? Besides, the conference attendees were enjoying the vendor area.

She and Laura took the staircase off the Main Hall, passing other guests trooping down. As they reached the top, Faith gazed around curiously. Behind them was the corridor running to the library stacks, and to their left, a railing overlooking the Great Hall Gallery. The milling crowd had diminished since workshops and seminars had begun.

"This way," Laura said, indicating a doorway opposite. "The bedrooms are on the other side of the lounge."

A door hidden in the paneling behind them opened and Wolfe emerged, startling Faith and Laura, who shrieked and jumped. Wolfe appeared unfazed. "Good morning, ladies." His blue eyes crinkled in a smile. "Sorry to scare you."

Cheeks flaming, Laura ducked her head in a nod. "Good morning, Mr. Jaxon."

"Hi, Wolfe." Faith felt her own face heat up, her feelings warring between friendship and suspicion. *If he wasn't so darn good-looking, that would help.* And did he routinely use the secret passages in the mansion? She wondered if a map of them was available.

"Faith, I'm glad I caught you," he said, to her surprise. "I'm hosting a private reception tonight for the conference speakers and I'd like you to come."

Laura squealed. "You should go. I saw the menu and it's awesome." She clapped a hand over her mouth, but Wolfe threw her a dazzling smile.

"It *is* awesome. I should know, I selected it." He adjusted his tie. "So what do you say?"

What could she say? Her boss wanted her to attend. "I'd love to. Thanks."

"Six o'clock." He began to head down the next flight of stairs. "On the third floor. See you then."

As he descended out of sight down the stairs, Laura threw her an envious glance. "You are so lucky. He's the hottest boss I ever had." She sighed. "I wish he'd ask *me* on a date."

Wolfe was the "hottest" boss Faith had ever worked for as well, but that wasn't the point. "I think it's a work thing," she said, "not a date." Although the way her heart leaped when he stopped to talk . . . Faith firmly put her unruly thoughts into order. Until the mystery of Doris's death was solved, it was better to keep Wolfe at arm's length, figuratively *and* literally.

The maid led Faith through a long sitting room that corresponded to the Main Hall downstairs and into a hallway circuiting the second floor. They passed door after door, all of them closed.

"How many guest bedrooms are there?" she asked Laura.

"Nineteen." Laura gave a rueful laugh. "And I've cleaned them all."

"It seems like there are more people here than could be staying in those rooms." Faith had the sense the conference was hosting close to a hundred.

"Some people are coming in for the day or staying nearby. Most of our events aren't quite this big." Laura sighed. "Thank goodness."

Thank goodness is right. No wonder the library had been packed this week, although the murder had only boosted interest. When she was hired, Faith had pictured smaller, more intimate gatherings.

They reached the east end of the mansion and Laura tapped on a door. "I'm going to check out the mess first and then I'll fetch the cleaning cart."

Benedict answered, for once not wearing his deerstalker cap, and Faith was pleasantly surprised to see he had a nice head of brown hair. He raised his brows at seeing her. "Do librarians make house calls too?"

"Only in case of book emergencies," Faith said. She moved into the room, struck by the sense of stepping into a fantasy. The wood-paneled room was decorated like a luxury train compartment. The furniture was gold brocade; the lamps, Tiffany; and the four-poster bed was hung with curtains.

"You should see the bathroom," Laura said. "There's a marble tub and an Egyptian mummy. Fake, of course."

Faith spotted Midge sitting with Molly on one of the sofas in front of the marble fireplace, under the gaze of Dame Agatha Christie. "How is she?"

Midge stroked her head. "She'll be fine in a day or so. She got into something that didn't agree with her."

Laura went to a wet area of the burgundy Persian rug and knelt down to peer at it.

"I tried to clean it up," Benedict said, "but I think it should be treated with stain remover."

The maid hopped up. "I'll be right back." She bustled out of the room, the door banging behind her. Benedict winced and shook his head, then sat in an armchair next to Midge.

Faith perched on another sofa. On the end table was a box holding pairs of cuff links placed in tiny compartments. Her gaze went to a section holding a lone cuff link. It looked similar to the Sherlock Holmes head Watson found at the cottage, but she couldn't quite tell. She sat up straight and craned her neck, trying to get a better look.

"You can start Molly on a bland meal tomorrow morning," Midge was saying. "Today, offer her small drinks of water every hour or so."

"Should I worry if she doesn't drink? Sometimes she doesn't want to after she's been ill."

"Only if several hours go by—"

Tuning out, Faith stealthily shifted her seat closer to the end of the sofa. Seeing that the other two were engrossed in conversation, she reached over and pulled the box closer. Then she turned the lone cuff link so she could see it better.

Aha. It was exactly the same as the one Watson found. When had Sinclaire been in the cottage? And even more important, why had he downplayed his relationship to Doris?

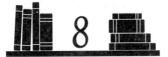

8

"Is there anything I can help you with?" Benedict's voice startled Faith, and she thrust the box of cuff links away, guilt making her flush with shame. How mortifying to be caught snooping.

"I'm sorry, I was looking at your cuff link collection. You have some extraordinary ones."

Benedict thrust out his sleeves to display the ones he was wearing, a pair of gold horse heads set with diamond eyes. "Collecting them is a hobby of mine."

"Nice." Faith nodded, feigning admiration. Inwardly she sighed with relief at her success at handling an awkward situation.

Midge rose. "Do you have any other questions before I leave, Benedict?"

Benedict plopped down beside Molly and gathered her onto his lap. "No, I think I'm all set, thank you." He bent his head toward his pet. "We're fine now that the nice vet came, aren't we?" The dog raised her head and licked his chin; it was an endearing sight.

The vet moved toward the door. "Call me if you have any questions or concerns—day or night. You have my cell."

"I'll do that, don't you worry."

"I'll walk you downstairs," Faith said. "See you later, Mr. Sinclaire."

Outside the door, Faith exhaled with a sigh, letting her shoulders slump. "That was embarrassing."

Midge cocked a brow. "You aren't a cuff link freak, are you?" she asked drily. They began walking down the hall side by side.

"No, I'm not." Faith glanced around. No one was in sight. "I found a cuff link at the cottage that matches one he has in his collection—that lacks a mate, by the way."

"So you think he lost it there? What does that mean?"

Faith shrugged. "Probably nothing. He denies knowing Doris but obviously he was in her house at some point." She shook her head. "The worst thing about murder is it puts everyone under the microscope." Her cell phone rang, and when she pulled it out to check the number, her heart thumped in shock. "Eek. The police are calling."

"You'd better take it." Midge's face creased in concern. "Although I can't imagine what they want."

Faith attempted a laugh. "Like I said, we're all under the microscope. Including me."

This time the police asked her to come down to the station. Fortunately they were willing to wait until her lunch break. The last thing Faith wanted to do was ask for time off during a busy conference to be questioned by the police.

The Lighthouse Bay Police Station was a fairly new white clapboard Cape Cod designed to blend in with the local architecture. The only thing that gave away its purpose were the cruisers parked out back and the antennas on the roof.

The resemblance to a historic home ended as soon as Faith entered the small front vestibule. Through the glass door, she saw the interior was stripped down and plain. Behind a waist-high counter with a glass window was an open area holding several desks.

"Can I help you?" The woman at the front desk peered at Faith over her tortoiseshell glasses. In her midforties, she was attractive, with shoulder-length blonde hair and perfect makeup. A nameplate in the window read, *Daphne Kerrigan*.

Faith shifted from foot to foot, mortified at the situation. "I'm Faith Newberry. Officer Rooney called me."

Pursing her full red lips, Daphne looked Faith up and down. "Oh yes. Take a seat and she'll come get you."

Faith sat in one of the orange plastic chairs lining the front hallway, hoping they wouldn't make her wait too long. She might be late opening the library after lunch, and that wouldn't go over well with Marlene.

She gazed around the quiet station, wishing she had brought a book. There wasn't much to look at beyond a bulletin board crammed with public service notices, a wall clock, and the receptionist. Daphne kept glancing at her, no doubt curious about the new librarian—and murder suspect—at Castleton Manor. Under other circumstances, Daphne might have been a new friend.

Officer Rooney opened a door at the end of the hallway. "Miss Newberry? Come this way."

Feeling a dread even stronger than that caused by a visit to the dentist for a filling, Faith stood and walked down the hallway, her heels tapping on the shiny tile. Maybe she should have called an attorney. *But isn't that something guilty people do?* She sucked air into her constricted lungs. *Calm down, Faith. Listen carefully and answer only the questions they ask.*

Once again, Faith was questioned by the amiable Mick Tobin and the prickly Jan Rooney. *Good cop, mean cop.*

They sat in a tiny room with no windows. A video camera near the ceiling winked when Rooney picked up the control. "May we videotape this interview?" Rooney asked.

"Of course." Faith attempted a laugh. "You should have warned me; I would have freshened my makeup."

Her joke fell flat, although Tobin did crack a small smile. "Thank you for coming down, Miss Newberry," Tobin said. He shuffled through a file of papers. "We have a few more questions for you."

"No problem. Fire away."

Rooney pounced. "So until you were hired, you never went to Castleton Manor?"

"That's right. The first interview was held in Boston, at Wolfe Jaxon's office. After they called me and asked if I wanted the job, I came over and toured the place. That was about a week and a half ago." *Is that really as long as it's been?* It felt like centuries since she had accepted the job and moved in.

"You're absolutely sure of that?" Rooney narrowed her eyes, staring so intensely at Faith that she felt her cheeks heat up.

Was she? For a brief moment of blind panic she thought maybe she had been there and had forgotten somehow. No, she remembered perfectly the first time she had seen the mansion library—and met Marlene. How could she forget either? "Yes, I'm sure."

Tobin glanced at his papers again. "You drive a silver 2012 Honda CRV?"

"That's right, I do." *What else do they know about me? My shoe size?*

"We have a witness who saw you on the road to Castleton on Saturday of Labor Day weekend," Rooney said. "Was there a reason you were on that road?"

Faith slumped in relief. That was all they had? "Actually, I did go that way. I took it as a shortcut to my aunt's house." She favored that route since it took her past Castleton Manor and several other gorgeous mansions.

"Any particular reason?" Rooney's tone was biting.

"I like it. I love old summerhouses." Faith shrugged. "And by the traffic on that road, I'm guessing a lot of other people do too." In fact, that street was recommended on a local map for sightseers.

"Where did you go after that?" Tobin's tone was kind and Faith sensed he believed her.

"To my aunt's and then out to lunch for lobster rolls." Faith took them through the fairly dull movements of her day. Feeling encouraged by the release of tension she sensed once she completed her recitation, she added, "I had no idea the secret chamber existed. So how could I have killed Doris in there?" She was going against her own decision to keep quiet but she couldn't help herself. The whole thing was too ridiculous and she wanted it resolved.

"Who says she was killed in the secret room?" Rooney blurted. The officer's cheeks reddened and she bit her lip, apparently regretting her outburst.

Tobin frowned at his colleague. "Forget you heard that, Miss Newberry. You can go."

"So that's all they had? Someone saw you driving by the manor?" Brooke shook her head with a sigh. "Pathetic. They're going to need more than that." She flipped through the hangers in Faith's closet, searching for the perfect outfit for the reception. Faith had called upon her new friend for advice.

"I did learn something new. Doris wasn't killed in the secret room. The killer hid her body there."

"Really? After all these weeks they're going to have trouble finding evidence anywhere." Brooke pulled out a silver spangled knee-length skirt and shook it at Faith. "Wear this. It's perfect."

"It's not too dressy?" Faith last wore the skirt on New Year's Eve.

"Nope. Not with this soft black sweater." The one Brooke selected had bell sleeves and a scoop neck. "And these shoes." Black velvet pumps.

After Faith laid out the clothes, she had to agree the outfit was attractive and hit the perfect note for the party. "Will you be my personal stylist? That only took you about five minutes."

Brooke laughed. "Clothes are my second passion, after cooking."

She patted her slim tummy. "Unfortunately they sometimes work against each other."

"Not in your case." Faith glanced at the clock. "Uh-oh. It's five already. I'd better hop in the shower."

"And I'd better get back to the kitchen. I've been drafted to help serve tonight."

"I wouldn't have dragged you over here if I'd known you had to work." Faith opened her bureau drawer and fished around for a fresh pair of nylons.

"No problem. Besides, I wanted to hear the update with the police." Impulsively, Brooke gave Faith a hug. "We're going to find the real killer, don't you worry. I won't let them railroad you."

Brooke's warmth touched Faith and she gave her a squeeze back. "Not even if Bryan Laddy is the arresting officer?"

Brooke faked a swoon. "Not even." She headed for the doorway. "See you in a few." She whirled around and gave Faith a thumbs-up. "Knock 'em dead. Oh, I should say, knock 'em out." With a laugh, she ran out of the room.

Faith turned to Watson, who was sitting on the window seat. "Good friends make all the difference, don't they, Watson? I'm grateful for that mercy anyway."

Watson blinked, the stump of his tail flicking back and forth.

"Don't worry, you're still my best pal." Faith laughed as she shut the bureau drawer. Her cell rang and she glanced at it curiously. *Wolfe.* What on earth could he want?

"Faith." Wolfe's tone was warm. "Can you come over a little early? I'd like to give you a tour before the others get here."

Faith agreed; then, after hanging up, she yelped and dashed for the shower. Her hour to get ready had dwindled to thirty minutes.

"Welcome to my lair." Wolfe grinned at Faith, waving the unlit meerschaum pipe he held. "Glad you could make it."

"Has Sherlock fever gripped you too?" With amusement, Faith eyed the pipe and the plaid cape he wore.

"I was trying these on for the costume ball at the end of the week." He handed Faith the pipe and pulled off the cape and hung it in a closet. "Not all of the groups dress up but it's fun when they do. Adds a little drama to our events."

"I'm looking forward to a gathering of science-fiction fans then." Faith laughed, picturing guests dressed like space aliens and astronauts.

Wolfe wagged a finger at her. "Don't laugh. They know how to rock a costume." He led the way out of the vestibule into a large living room lined with tall windows.

Faith gasped at the view of the ocean, stunning anytime, no doubt, but spectacular right now as the setting sun turned the sky orange, pink, and gold.

"Isn't it gorgeous?" Wolfe joined her at the window. "I could leave this room totally bare and no one would notice."

Faith tore her eyes away from the view, taking in the elegant late 1800s furniture, oriental rugs, and crystal chandeliers. "I don't know about that. Your place is gorgeous."

"Thanks. Furnished by my great-great-grandparents, and nothing's been changed." He grinned. "Except the kitchen and bathrooms. I had to insist those be updated." He gestured. "Come on, I'll show you around."

The first rooms he showed her were the private family library and his personal office. Here as in the library, bookshelves were crammed with luscious, old leather-bound volumes, many of them first editions, Faith noticed. It was mind-boggling that on top of the fabulous collection downstairs, they would have additional valuable books up here.

With an inward sigh, she turned her attention from the books to Wolfe's personal belongings. She really needed to do some investigating while she had the opportunity. She noticed that there was a desk calendar on his desk, open to the month of September. She really should get a closer look at that, if possible. Pretending interest in a photograph of a racing sailboat over the mantel, she edged closer. "Are you a sailor?"

"I certainly am. That's a picture of me sailing in a knockabout race when I was thirteen. My first win. I still take that boat out quite often. She's small and nimble. Eighteen feet."

"Really? That's quite small." Faith was surprised, figuring someone of Wolfe's wealth would own huge, expensive boats.

"It is, relatively speaking. I also have a forty-foot cabin sailboat for long trips and a yacht." He showed her photographs from the desk.

Faith also noticed a photograph of a pretty, blonde young woman with elegant cheekbones and green eyes. Did he have a girlfriend?

Before she could avert her gaze, Wolfe noticed her looking at the studio portrait. He picked it up and gazed at it sadly. "This is my fiancée, Valentina Pestova. Or I should say, my late fiancée." He shook his head. "I still can't believe she's gone."

"I'm so sorry, Wolfe," Faith said softly. "She was beautiful."

Wolfe set the photograph down. "She was." He sighed. "She was a very talented swimsuit model and designer."

A perfect mate for a handsome millionaire. Faith didn't want to probe and she was mortified that she had reminded Wolfe—albeit inadvertently—of his loss, but she wondered what had taken the lovely young woman's life.

Wolfe apparently didn't mind talking about it. "She fell off my yacht during a party and drowned."

Faith repressed a gasp of shock. How horrible. As she scrambled for something to say, she was rescued by Brooke's appearance in the doorway.

"I'm sorry to interrupt, Mr. Jaxon, but I wanted to let you know that we're all set up and ready to go." Brooke slid Faith a smile, glancing up and down her apparel in approval.

"Thanks, Brooke. Station someone at the door, will you? The other guests should be arriving soon. I'm giving our new librarian a tour."

"Will do, Mr. Jaxon." Brooke grinned at them. "Enjoy the tour, Faith. This place is fantastic."

Faith hoped Wolfe didn't notice the subtext in the cheeky chef's words and attitude. Discussing the lost love of his life was about the furthest thing from romantic intrigue she could imagine. Plus she had other motives for spending time with her boss. With one final glance at the desk calendar, she allowed Wolfe to usher her from the room. She was almost certain she saw the notation *Doris* on the Friday before Labor Day weekend. Somehow she had to get back and confirm that.

They barely had a chance to glance at the billiards room, private gym, gun room, and walk-in cigar humidor before guests were thronging the other living room. At one end, tables and a beverage service station had been set up, and in addition, servers were circulating with trays.

"Bacon-wrapped scallop?" Laura held out a tray, the goodies sliding to one side. She quickly righted it.

"Thanks." Faith smiled as she selected one. *Delicious.* It melted in her mouth.

"Good, huh?" Laura smiled and tottered away, moving awkwardly on heels.

Faith shook her head. *That woman really shouldn't be wearing anything taller than flats.*

"There are some people I'd like you to meet," Wolfe said. Grateful for his company, Faith tagged along as their host greeted speakers, conference leaders, and other guests. Wolfe introduced her nicely and with seeming pride as she met an acclaimed authority who offered expertise to Hollywood films on Sherlock, a woman who had published a series with a female Holmes (Sherlock's sister), and a professor who used the novels in teaching investigation techniques to fledgling police officers. This last handed Faith his card, which included a Holmes quote and a silhouette of the detective.

All the while, Faith's mind was on Wolfe's office at the end of the apartment, but she couldn't figure out an excuse to go back there. Even when she requested directions to a restroom, she was directed to the facility near the gym, which was unfortunately available. After the crowd thinned, she was about to give up and go home when the conference organizers and Wolfe decided to look at Wolfe's book collection. She managed to tag along. For once, Benedict's companion Molly wasn't with him, and Faith hoped the little dog was doing all right. Deb, the deerstalker lady, had also left Clancy in her room.

"I've got a rabid case of bibliomania," Deb said. "I call it extreme book collecting."

"I've heard about people like you," Sandra said. "Isn't that categorized as a mental disorder?"

Deb flushed. "No, not officially. Besides, I only collect the cream of the crop and I always get rid of duplicates. So that's healthy, right?"

Sandra laughed. "If you say so. As long as you don't kill people for their books, like that Spanish monk in the 1800s."

An unpleasant thought jolted Faith. Was a book the motive for Doris's murder? That fake first edition, maybe? Or something else she didn't know about?

"Ladies, ladies." Benedict had obviously chosen the role of moderator for the group. "I think we can safely admit we're all a little nuts on the subject of books."

"I am," Faith said. "Why else would I be a librarian? My world is books, books, books, all the time."

The two women gave her startled looks, as if they hadn't seen her trailing behind them.

"That's why we hired you," Wolfe said. "Dedicated obsession." He winked at Faith as he stood back to let the others pass him and enter the library.

Why was he so nice? Faith felt as lowly as a worm for classifying him as a suspect. Then she remembered the police inquiries she'd had to endure. What had the professor's card said? Oh, yes, "Do not theorize before gathering data." That's all she was doing—collecting information, purely in self-defense.

Inside the private library the group broke up and began to examine the shelves, led by Wolfe proudly displaying the contents of his bookshelves. *How nutty about books is he?* she wondered. Not only did he have an amazing library that he shared with the retreat guests, but he also had a very select private collection.

Faith glanced at the open office door. So near and yet so far. She sidled up to Deb, who was avidly examining a Hemingway. "There's a first of *The Old Man and the Sea* in the office," Faith said. "In fact, all the books in there have nautical themes." She'd managed to notice that earlier. They had gone with the nautical decor.

Deb straightened as though galvanized by her remark. "They're arranged by theme? What an excellent way to organize books. I've done it by author, by period, by style . . . wow." She gently replaced the book on the shelf. "Let's go."

Too easy. Dangling books in front of a bibliophile was like tempting a child with candy. Faith led the way to the office, glancing over her shoulder to see if anyone noticed. The other three were in close conversation on the other side of the room.

"Here you go," she said to Deb, as if it were her library. Deb clapped her hands and gazed around, then beelined to something that caught her eye. While she *oohed* and *ahhed*, Faith slipped behind the desk.

As she thought, *Doris Lincoln* was written on the calendar, as a 4 p.m. appointment on the Friday before Labor Day. What had Doris and Wolfe discussed? Had Doris mentioned the forged *A Study in Scarlet*, or had there been another issue of concern?

She had no evidence, of course, that Doris had known about the fake book. She was only surmising based on her own expertise.

Voices approached the doorway and Faith quickly moved from behind the desk to the bookshelves. Reaching blindly, she grabbed a battered leather-bound volume and opened the front cover. Then she almost dropped it in surprise.

"Ship's Log—*SS Honoria*," someone had written in the flyleaf. Angus Jaxon's merchant ship, the one her ancestor was traveling on when he died.

9

"Find anything interesting?" Wolfe asked. His gaze fell on the ship's log Faith held. Before she could return it to the shelf, he moved forward and took it from her hands with a smile. "I'll show you that another time." He gently reshelved it.

Face flushing, Faith moved aside, wondering if he meant that. She thought of apologizing, but that might only make matters worse. She hadn't sought the ship's log out on purpose, but what were the chances he would believe her? Slim to none.

Fortunately Wolfe went to Deb's side and began to answer her questions about a volume of *Moby Dick*. Benedict and Sandra were engrossed in conversation, leaving Faith feeling like a fifth wheel. It was long past time to leave the party.

Faith cleared her throat. "Thanks again for inviting me," she said as Wolfe turned toward her. "It was wonderful." She nodded at the others. "See you tomorrow."

A chorus of "good nights" followed her across the library. She couldn't walk fast enough to escape her confusion and humiliation. Was Wolfe Jaxon what he appeared to be—urbane and charming, modest in spite of his wealth? Or was he a criminal who would stop at nothing to protect what he owned?

She had a terrible feeling Doris Lincoln might be able to answer that question.

On the way downstairs, Faith took a detour into the library. She remembered a section on architecture, along with some folios of historic house plans. What if Castleton Manor was among them? Maybe the plans would show the secret passageways Wolfe had alluded to.

The main floor of the mansion was quiet, although she heard the faint sound of revelry from the direction of the banquet hall. The guests must be having dinner. In the main gallery, only spotlights were on, leaving deep areas of darkness between them. Faith jumped a couple of times when she thought she saw a figure lurking behind a statue or standing near a tall piece of furniture.

This was foolish. One scream and dozens of people would come running. She wasn't here alone the way Doris had been when the retreat was closed. Well, alone except for a killer . . .

Reaching the library door, Faith gave a little bark of relief that echoed strangely, causing her to jump again. *Good grief, I don't have to worry about someone killing me. I'm going to scare myself to death.*

Inside the library, she locked the door and dashed around, turning on lamps. Then she scanned the shelves, seeking the architecture section. There it was. She searched through the portfolios, finally finding the *Castleton Manor Plans*, with the architectural firm and date inscribed below. Most ordinary people didn't have their plans bound, but she was grateful for this habit of the wealthy and influential. There was much to learn from the elaborate designs of the past.

Faith carried the binder to a long table and flipped it open. The first few pages showed elevations, drawings of various sides of the house. The next page was the floor plan for the basement.

A noise, a soft shuffling, attracted Faith's attention. *What was that?* She peered around the room, seeing nothing but silent shelves of books. The curtains hung straight and still, so a window hadn't been left open by accident. Then she heard the sound again, drawing her eyes upward.

Someone was on the balcony.

How she knew that, she really couldn't say. She couldn't see a soul. But a primitive instinct that made her hair stand on end told her that someone was staring down at her.

"Who's there?" she called, her voice wavering. *Ugh.* She really didn't want to betray how frightened she was.

No answer. She cleared her throat and tried again. "This isn't funny. Who's up there?"

Again, nothing. Gathering her courage in both hands, Faith strode across the floor. "I'm coming up," she called, her heart pounding. Why should she cower when the real coward was lurking in the shadows?

Another shuffle and a soft *bang*. The person had slipped out the upper door—which was supposed to be secured after hours. Faith stopped short. Had she locked it that afternoon? Angry at herself, she headed up the twisty stairs leading to the upper level. She'd been so distracted lately that she was becoming forgetful.

She took a deep breath, forcing herself to relax. Most likely the watcher was a curious guest, exploring. She'd probably looked like a maniac, yelling that way. But as Faith locked the door, she couldn't erase a niggling feeling that told her the intruder hadn't been an innocent observer.

Faith lugged the portfolio back to the cottage after remembering Wolfe's invitation when she was hired to freely use the library's resources. She wasn't quite sure if taking something home was what he meant, but she could clear it with him later. In any case, she would keep the plans only long enough to find where the secret passageways and doors were located.

Watson greeted her eagerly, rubbing against her legs and mewing piteously, as if she had been gone for weeks, not hours. She thumped the portfolio on the dining room table and bent to pat him. "I know, Rumpy. How about some you and me time? I'll make hot chocolate." He purred loudly in response.

Not that Watson drank hot chocolate, but he seemed to regard it as the signal for relaxation, the way she did. She kicked off her pumps and headed for the kitchen. Her preference was for the kind of cocoa made from scratch, using milk and sugar plus a touch of vanilla and cinnamon. While the milk heated, she put together a plate of cheese and crackers and a sliced apple. It had been awhile since she'd eaten those appetizers, and although she wasn't hungry enough for a full meal, she could use a snack. She added a few tuna treats for Watson.

Upstairs, cat at her heels, Faith set down the treat. First she peeled out of the constricting outfit and changed into the comfy flannels. After taking off her makeup, washing up, and brushing her hair, she climbed into bed, with Watson jumping up beside her. One of the windows was open to the night air, the soothing, regular sound of the breakers wafting in.

"This is nice, isn't it, Rumpy?" She fed him a treat and then popped a cracker topped with cheese and apple into her mouth. Owner and cat crunched contentedly.

As she sipped her hot chocolate, Faith allowed the peace of the quiet evening to wash over her. A bright ray of hope stole through the confusing storm clouds in her mind and heart. Maybe, just maybe, everything would be resolved and she and Watson could finally enjoy their new home.

A rapping on the front door woke her early, early enough that the pink of dawn still tinted the sky. Faith sat bolt upright. Surely Marlene wouldn't come over here this early? Sighing, she hopped out of bed and tied on a robe. Whoever it was would have to take her the way she was, like it or not.

Officer Rooney appeared not to like it. "Miss Newberry?" Her lips curled as she scanned Faith's outfit. "We've got a search warrant for the cottage and grounds."

"You're searching the cottage? But why?" Faith blinked, wondering if she was still asleep and having a bad dream. "There's nothing of Doris's here. Or anyone else's, either, for that matter." She remembered the cuff link. "Except a cuff link my cat found."

"A cuff link?" Rooney almost laughed, but she quickly straightened out her face. She waved a piece of paper at Faith. "Here's the warrant if you want to see it." She gestured to Officers Tobin and Laddy, standing behind her. "Come on, let's go."

With apologetic shrugs, the two men shouldered past Faith, following Rooney into the cottage. After watching them tornado through the living room for a few minutes, lifting sofa cushions and searching through books and drawers, even behind paintings, Faith went to the kitchen to make coffee and feed Watson.

Jan Rooney appeared in the doorway as Faith was pulling a mug out of the cupboard. "Would you like a cup of coffee, Officer? I made plenty."

"No thanks." Officer Rooney shifted from foot to foot. "You mentioned a cuff link. We probably should take a look at it."

"Certainly. It's on the mantel." Faith set down the mug and went into the living room. Officer Tobin had moved on to the dining room and Faith heard footsteps overhead, which meant Officer Laddy was up there. She squirmed inwardly. He was actually going to paw through her clothing and personal belongings. *Ugh.*

Trying not to think about Laddy, she retrieved the cuff link and handed it to Rooney. "I'm sure it's covered with my prints. I didn't realize at first that it might belong to someone at the conference that's going on now."

Rooney's glance was sharp. "Why do you think that?"

"Because it's an image of Sherlock Holmes. And he's the focus of the conference."

"Oh, right. That's true." The officer pulled a small plastic bag out of her pocket and dropped the cuff link inside. "Thanks for this." Her tone was gruff, but Faith thought she heard a note of apology.

"Sure thing. I'm only trying to do my part." Even if that meant someone rummaging through her house.

Tobin popped out of the dining room. "You need to see this, Jan."

The officer followed him back into the room and Faith tagged along, wondering what he was talking about. Tobin pointed to the portfolio on the table.

"Aha. House plans for Castleton Manor." Rooney quirked a brow. "Where did those come from, Miss Newberry?"

Faith's mouth dried. Why hadn't she officially checked the book out or asked Wolfe for permission? "I brought it home from the manor library last night. I wanted to get better acquainted with the property."

Rooney laughed roughly, the earlier apologetic tone gone. "I'll bet. Like the secret passageways, for instance?"

Since that was exactly right, Faith couldn't rebut the officer's words. She felt her cheeks flame with embarrassment. "I didn't have access to it before Doris's death," she finally said. "And that's what counts, right?"

Rooney regarded her skeptically for a moment, then turned to Tobin. "Bag it."

Now she wouldn't have a chance to learn the secret routes through the mansion. Faith excused herself and fled to the kitchen, where she poured a cup of coffee with shaking hands. Things kept going from bad to worse. She couldn't look guiltier if she tried.

The trio of officers had now moved outdoors, and Faith heard shouts as they moved about the lawn and gardens. Watson jumped up on the window seat and watched, tail twitching.

"I'll be glad when they're gone too." Faith sat beside him on the seat, sipping her coffee. Now the men were wielding shovels while Rooney crashed around the bushes, yelling. "I wish she'd stop thinking I'm a murderer. We might actually be friends." There was a lively intelligence and gutsiness about the officer that Faith liked.

Laddy yelled and then began to chop at the soil under a bush, the one where Faith—or rather, Watson—had found Doris's purse. The other two came to watch him work. After a few more strokes of the shovel, he bent to pick something up.

Faith gasped and even Watson's eyes grew wide. Laddy held a fireplace poker in his gloved hands.

10

The officers tested the poker with their analysis kit, and by the grim looks on their faces, Faith guessed the murder weapon had been found. Someone had used the fireplace poker to kill Doris. Had they done it right here, in this room? She shivered and clutched Watson close. In response, he touched her face gently with a paw.

"You're the best, Watson." She smooched his soft, furry head.

Glancing up, Officer Rooney saw Faith peering out the window and came storming for the front door. Faith was ready for her and opened it before she knocked.

"Oh." Officer Rooney lowered her fist. "We've found some new evidence that means this cottage could be a crime scene. You'll have to clear out. But don't go far."

Faith's spirits sank even lower. "For how long?"

Rooney peered around, lips pursed. "For as long as it takes." She shrugged. "Depending on what we find, I'll let you know later. That's the best I can do."

"All right." Faith supposed she could stay with her aunt. It wasn't ideal since it meant a commute and displacing Watson but at least she had somewhere to go. "I'll be at the library today if you need to reach me."

"We have your number." With that, Rooney nodded and turned to leave.

Faith headed for the stairs. Her plan was to get dressed and head out early. The sooner she got out of the police's hair—or maybe them out of hers—the better. Maybe they would find something to exonerate her. She could only hope, right?

Watson at her heels, Faith slipped quickly through the Main Hall and the gallery to the library, thankful not to encounter a single soul. She really wasn't in the mood to talk to anyone. Maybe she could use the "quiet in the library" rule to avoid conversation today. She sighed. Not much chance of that. The retreat guests were nothing short of gregarious.

She unlocked the door and opened it wide to allow Watson to enter. She flipped a switch, then stopped dead in disbelief.

The entire fiction section had been removed from the shelves and placed on the floor in towering stacks.

Faith stared at the mess in disbelief, feeling anger stir. Who could have done this—and why? She had hours, absolute hours of work ahead.

The jingling of keys sounded as Marlene entered the library. "Good morning—oh my." The manager covered her smile with a hand. "I guess you've been punked."

"I'll say." Faith put her hands on her hips. "Who did this?"

Marlene shrugged. "I have no idea." She cocked her head. "Are you sure you locked up?"

"Of course. In fact—" Faith had been about to explain that she'd double-checked last night, but then she'd have to say why she had come into the library after hours. She wasn't going to tell Marlene she'd borrowed a book—a book that was now in police custody. She groaned in frustration.

"What was that?" Marlene's green eyes narrowed.

"I was going to say I always double-check." She thought of something. "Though with all the secret passageways in the mansion, maybe they came in that way."

Marlene's cheeks pinked. "Secret passageways?"

"There must be at least one. I saw Wolfe Jaxon come out a secret door on the second-floor landing. Right near the upstairs entrance to the library."

Rather than answer, the manager's eyes darted around the room, landing on Watson, who sat in a patch of sunlight, grooming. "You brought that animal again?"

"Why not? I was told he was welcome." Faith crossed her arms. She wasn't going to allow Marlene to brush off the annoying incident by changing the subject. "Are you going to help me put these books away? Otherwise the guests aren't really going to enjoy using the library today."

"Me?" Marlene stabbed her chest with a forefinger. "Oh no, I'm way too busy." She straightened. "I have a retreat to run."

"And I have a library to manage. So send someone right away, please." Faith's eyes met the assistant manager's and by an act of will, she stared until Marlene looked away first.

"All right. I'll do that as soon as I can." Marlene pivoted on her heel and tapped toward the door. "By the way, there's a high tea this afternoon, and I expect you to attend," she called over her shoulder.

"Whatever you say, your highness," Faith muttered after she was sure the woman was out of earshot. Then she bit her lip. She shouldn't allow the stress and strain of what was going on to make her irritable. Marlene was difficult to get along with, but Faith still owed her respect.

Faith began to shelve the books, noticing that they weren't stacked in alphabetical order, which would have made the task much easier.

Laura bustled into the library. "Marlene told me you need some help in here." She stopped short. "Whoa. What happened?"

"I don't know, but I can tell you it wasn't my idea." Faith heard the tartness in her tone and softened it. "Thanks for coming to help. I can really use you." She smiled at the waitress. "Think of it as training for when you're a librarian. You'll need to be familiar with books."

"Thanks for the vote of confidence. I don't get many of those." Laura scanned the piles. "I have an idea. Why don't I pull out the *A*'s and you can shelve them in order. Then we'll do *B* and so on."

Faith was impressed. "Great idea, especially since I don't know how many books we have under each letter of the alphabet."

They worked together in silence for a while, developing an easy rhythm. "This is almost fun," Laura said with a laugh. "Plus I'm seeing lots of books I'd like to read."

Faith was too. The mansion's collection could only be termed eclectic, with fiction from every era from the 1700s through the present day.

"Have you worked at the retreat long?" Faith asked, hoping to work around to discussing Doris without being blatant about it.

"A few months. Before that, I worked in town, in a bookshop."

"Franklin Woodbury's shop?"

Laura kept her gaze on her task. "Yep. It didn't work out. And before that, I worked for a photographer. But he left town." She shrugged. "I guess I haven't found my niche."

"Maybe I can figure something out, give you some hours in here." Faith bit her tongue. That was a rash offer. "I'll have to clear it with Wolfe and Marlene first, though."

Laura's face lit up. "I'd love that, thanks."

Faith got the discussion back on track. "I have to admit I'm curious about my predecessor, Doris. You told me before that she tried to get you fired, but what was she like?" Again she felt a stab of guilt for gossiping. But how else was she going to figure out what had happened to the librarian?

Pursing her lips, Laura shook her head. "Not that nice, to be honest. It was her way or the highway."

"Kind of like Marlene," Faith blurted. She slapped a hand to her mouth. "Did I say that? Sorry. It was out of line."

Laura leaned close. "That's just it, they were both the same, wanting their own way about everything." She knocked her fists together. "Always butting heads."

Faith studied the young woman. She needed to tread delicately.

"Was there anything in particular that was upsetting her that last week?"

"What wasn't bothering her?" Laura crossed her arms tightly. "She thought someone stole a book. And she even accused me. As if."

Faith's pulse jumped. Here was a real clue at last. "Do you remember which book?" Faith made an attempt to keep eagerness out of her voice.

Laura shrugged. "One of those Sherlock Holmes novels. I was helping sort books for the library sale, so I think that's why she thought I took it. Otherwise I barely ever came in here. She also told me not to talk to anyone about the missing book, since she was going to handle it."

"What day was that?" Faith asked. "Do you remember?"

"I certainly do. Friday morning before Labor Day."

Faith thought about the notation on Wolfe's calendar for a meeting with Doris that afternoon. Had Doris told him then about the forged book? She glanced at the locked case, where the false *A Study in Scarlet* sat. If so, why was it still on display? With a sinking feeling, she realized only one answer fit. *He wanted it there.*

After they finished shelving the fiction, Laura went back to her maid duties and Faith opened the library for visitors. After a busy morning, she decided to have lunch in the dining room since the cottage was still off-limits as far as she knew.

As she strode through the gallery, noticing that the vendors were back, her phone rang. Lighthouse Bay PD. Ducking into a quiet alcove behind the Agatha Christie statue, Faith stared at the number, her heart pounding. Were they finally going to arrest her? But surely they'd arrive in person to do that. She pictured herself being cuffed in front of the library patrons. How humiliating. Gritting her teeth, she answered.

"Miss Newberry?" It was Officer Tobin. "I wanted to give you an update. You'll be able to get back into the cottage tonight, after we release the scene."

That was all? Relief rushed through her limbs, making her weak. "That's great. Did you . . . find anything?"

"Um . . ." Tobin cleared his throat. "I really can't say. But you'll be all set later. Someone will call you."

Faith thanked him and hung up. He'd been about to tell her more, she sensed, but he probably wasn't allowed to share information with suspects. Faith groaned as she tucked her phone into her bag. She almost succumbed to despair, but then, as she glanced up at the Dame of Mystery's wise, calm face, she rallied. She should allow her fear to propel her forward, into solving the mystery, rather than wallowing in miserable apprehension.

After a quick bowl of fish chowder, Faith went back to the library, where she spent a hectic afternoon. She barely had time to spare a thought for Doris, the state of her cottage, or the forged book situation. The police hadn't called by the time the high tea started, so Faith decided to obey Marlene and attend.

"Take a seat anywhere," the server at the door said.

Faith glanced around the dining room. Each table was covered with a white cloth and held tiers of sandwiches and treats and flowers. Other servers were going around with tea carts, taking orders and providing tiny teapots full of steaming water. Many of the guests were in costume, this group apparently seizing on any opportunity to dress in period-appropriate outfits.

Near the front, she saw Deb and Sandra at a table and decided to sit with them. Ever since she'd noticed Deb's avid interest in book collecting, she'd wanted to talk to her further. The tea might provide a perfect, casual excuse.

"How goes library world?" Deb asked as Faith took a seat, followed by Watson. The other woman covertly fed a triangle sandwich to Clancy, who was lying under the table. Gulping the sandwich, the dog gave

Watson a wide-eyed look that subsided when the cat ignored him in favor of jumping up to an empty chair.

"It's great, thank you." Faith didn't mention the prank she'd spent the morning fixing. "How's the conference going?" With all that had been on her mind, she hadn't been involved beyond her duties.

"Even better than we hoped." Sandra cast a glance around the room at the chattering, laughing group. "Everyone seems to be having a wonderful time."

"You've done a masterful job of planning." Faith's remark was heartfelt. It took a great deal of work to make an event like this run smoothly.

"We're a good team," Deb said. "Benedict and the two of us worked closely together from start to finish."

Faith picked up the menu at her place setting. The offerings included cucumber with aioli and chives, smoked salmon with cream cheese, and egg salad and watercress. One of each for her and a smoked salmon for Watson. The server rolled up a cart and gave her a Darjeeling tea bag for her hot water.

"Benedict writes mystery novels, right?" Faith asked once the server left. She took a bite of the cucumber sandwich and almost moaned. It was so good.

"Yes," Deb said, "historical mysteries featuring Watson."

At the mention of his name, Watson lifted his head. Faith reached out and patted him. "Not you, although you do deserve a book series."

Deb picked up on the joke. "Maybe he and Clancy could work together, as detectives." She lifted the cloth to peer under the table. "What do you think of that, boy?"

Watson's expression at this idea could only be called disgruntled. Faith laughed and fed him another piece of salmon. "Don't worry, you won't have to share top billing."

Sandra shook her head. "You two and your pets. You must think they understand what you're saying."

Faith and Deb looked at each other. "They do," they said in unison. Sandra rolled her eyes and took a sip of tea.

"What do you do?" Faith asked Deb. "When you're not planning events, that is."

Deb shrugged. "Not much. I'm a trust fund baby."

"Don't let her fool you," Sandra said. "She does tons for charity. In fact, she sponsored a children's program at the library where I work in inner-city Boston."

Deb grunted and focused on her sandwich, her cheeks burning.

"That's wonderful," Faith said. Then she absorbed the rest of Sandra's words. "You're a librarian?"

"I sure am. Twenty years and counting." Sandra's smile was prideful. "And I love it as much now as I did when I started."

"That librarian who got killed worked with you, right, Sandra?" Deb said.

"Doris Lincoln?" Faith's ears perked up. She didn't know anything about Doris's time before Lighthouse Bay. Was the librarian's murder connected to something that happened in a former life?

Sandra's face was somber. "That's right, Doris worked with me. She was a librarian at one of our biggest branches."

That must be why Doris had edged her out—experience at a larger library. "Did you know Doris well?" Faith asked.

Instead of answering, Sandra flagged down a passing server and asked for a refill of hot water and a tea choice. By the time he moved away, the moment had passed.

Had Sandra's avoidance been deliberate? Maybe Faith should look into her predecessor's background and see if there was anything of interest. She hadn't even thought to do that.

Later, after Watson and Faith had eaten their fill and were groaning with repletion, they walked back to the cottage. The awaited call from Officer Tobin had finally come, telling her she was cleared to go home. Night had fallen, more evidence the days were getting shorter as the calendar moved toward winter. Halfway through the garden, Faith heard footsteps crunching on the gravel path behind. She glanced over her shoulder, expecting to see a guest taking an evening stroll or an employee cutting over to the parking lot.

In the dim glow from a lamppost, she saw the outline of a figure wearing a cape.

Watson hissed, his hackles rising. Faith stared into the dark, trying to see who was following her. From this distance, in this light, she couldn't even tell if the figure was male or female. Maybe she was imagining things—but Watson's reaction told her otherwise.

Faith started moving again, footsteps quickening. Watson trotted beside her, eager to get to the safety of home.

The footsteps crunched again. Whirling around, Faith thought she saw the figure dart behind a tall, sculptured bush. Now she was really spooked. She still hadn't recovered from her strange experience in the library, where another watcher had stared at her out of the shadows.

"Come on, Watson. I'll race you home." Grateful she was wearing flats for once, Faith broke into a run. Watson darted past, his body stretching out into a lope. He beat her to the front steps and sat waiting as she dug out her keys on the fly.

Thankful she'd left the outside light burning, she hustled Watson inside, then locked and bolted the door. Putting her face to the window, she peered outside to see if the person had followed them.

She saw nothing except the effects of a sudden breeze that tossed the trees and bushes near the cottage.

Is he watching? Faith ran from window to window, yanking the curtains closed. *Now what?* Hugging herself, she glanced at the fireplace, tempted to build a fire to chase away her bone-deep chill.

The missing poker. Faith shuddered, remembering why the poker was gone, used to . . . With a huge effort, she steeled her spine in resolve. She couldn't—wouldn't— allow evildoers to sour her life. She gave a brave but warbling whistle. "Come on, Watson," she called. "Let's get cozy."

Although warm and relaxed after reading mindless fluff by the fire for a couple of hours, Faith's tensions and fears returned as soon as she slid into bed. She lay staring at the ceiling, noticing how dark it was on the manor grounds. In Boston, no matter how late the hour, there had always been car lights sliding over the ceiling and the glow of city lights brightening the sky.

To distract herself, she thought about the gardener who lived here when the mansion was built, the man responsible for creating the incredible gardens. Did he have a family? She pictured a lively bunch of boys and girls seated around the long dining room table downstairs, laughing and chatting as they passed bowls and plates around. Or maybe he had been an elderly man, alone in the cottage with his wife, the two of them spending winter days by the fire while she knitted and he smoked a pipe and dreamed of the gardens in spring.

Either way, the women of the house must have had difficulty cramming those long dresses into the cottage's tiny closets. Maybe they used wardrobes or armoires instead.

Her pleasant musings fled as realization struck. Where in the world were Doris's clothing and personal items? Murder victims didn't neatly dispose of their possessions before they died, so everything should have been in the cottage that Tuesday after Labor Day. Unless . . . maybe Doris had quit, put her things in storage, and then been killed before she could leave. Either way, her belongings had to be somewhere. If Faith could find them, maybe they would provide a clue to whoever killed her—and why.

Due to broken sleep and bad dreams, Faith slept late, grateful she didn't have to go to the library until after lunch. Her hours varied each week according to the needs of the guests. Around nine, Watson let her know she'd slept long enough by a discreet yowl in her ear. She reluctantly pulled herself out of bed.

After breakfast, she sat down with a second cup of coffee at her laptop to start researching. She opened a browser and typed *Doris Lincoln Massachusetts librarian* into the search bar. Her heart sank. The murder had finally made the local news. "Librarian checks out," screamed one tabloid headline. "Final edition for this librarian," read another. Her pulse pounding, Faith scanned the articles, searching for her name. She wasn't mentioned in any of them, thank goodness.

"The death has been ruled foul play," Chief Garris was quoted as saying, "and we're following a number of leads." Good. At least he hadn't said they were questioning a "person of interest," which was one step away from being a suspect.

After reading her fill about the case, Faith moved on to learning about Doris when she was alive. She found her on a couple of social media sites, including a professional one that listed her credentials and displayed a nice head shot. With short hair, eyeglasses, and a slightly stern expression, Doris appeared to be the stereotypical librarian.

On an impulse, Faith searched for Marlene Russell on the site, curious to learn about her background. Before becoming retreat assistant manager, Marlene managed a high-end oceanfront lodging property and restaurant next to the local yacht club. Maybe she met Wolfe there and that's how she got the job at Castleton Manor.

Moving back to Doris Lincoln, Faith found a personal social media page that showed a more playful side. She favored cute pictures and videos of cats, which touched Faith. Would they have been friends, perhaps? Doris's interests included kayaking, travel with friends, and exotic eating experiences. In many photos she was grinning ear to ear, clearly delighted with life.

And someone had cruelly cut her time short. A new determination stiffened Faith's spine. "I'll find out who did this, Doris, I promise," she whispered. Her quest for the truth had shifted from self-preservation to finding justice for a fellow librarian.

Faith read news articles featuring Doris when she was working in her former position at a city library. "Budget discussion turns contentious," read one article from earlier in the year. Apparently during the city's annual budget preparations, Doris asserted that the main library was overfunded at the expense of the branches.

Sandra Baker, head of the library system, refuted the claims. The situation degenerated into a heated public argument, according to the reporter. A later article headline read, "Library budget under scrutiny, director in hot seat." Apparently officials took action on Doris's complaints.

Faith checked the date on the articles. Doris left soon after to take the Castleton job. Voluntarily, or was she pushed out? Had Sandra held a grudge? Doris's complaints put Sandra in the spotlight and perhaps made her job situation tenuous in addition to being embarrassing. Library positions were scarce and job loss was no laughing matter. *Maybe Sandra came to see Doris at the retreat, they argued again, and* bam! *Sandra killed her.*

It was a plausible scenario. Benedict visited Castleton Manor in the weeks before Doris died. Had Sandra as well? Faith needed to find out.

Glancing at the time, she decided to have another cup of coffee before getting ready for work. In the kitchen, she thought again of Doris's missing possessions, and on impulse, picked up her cell and called the Lighthouse Bay Police Department.

Fortunately the dispatcher connected her to Bryan Laddy instead of Rooney or Tobin. "How can I help you?" Bryan's deep, pleasant voice was soothing.

"Officer Laddy, this is Faith Newberry."

Even through the phone line she sensed his sharpened attention. "Yes, Miss Newberry."

Faith took a deep breath. "I was thinking about Doris Lincoln's personal belongings."

"What about them?"

"Where are they?" In a rush, she added, "If she was planning to leave the retreat, then maybe she put them in storage. But if she didn't, someone else must have disposed of them after . . . after her death. There's nothing here in the cottage that belongs to her."

He thought about that for a minute. "Hmm. Interesting."

Encouraged, she said, "I was wondering if you found a storage unit key in her purse."

"I'm sorry, Miss Newberry, but I can't give you that information."

Had they even looked? Faith suspected the answer was no. If only she had noticed when she found the purse. But of course she hadn't known at that point that Doris was dead.

Officer Laddy clicked keys on his computer and she wondered if he was entering this information in the case notes. "Is there anything else, Miss Newberry?"

"No, not right now. But I'll call you if I think of something." She paused. "Or if I find Doris Lincoln's things."

"Don't go nosing around, Miss Newberry. Leave the investigating to the police."

So they could put her in jail? She didn't think so. But she deliberately made her tone meek. "Of course, Officer Laddy. I was only trying to help."

"We appreciate that. Have a good day."

Bemused, Faith hung up. She wasn't going to have a good day until this case was solved.

Later in the day, dressed for work, Faith stepped out into brilliant sunshine. A gentle ocean breeze carried the scent of salt and late-blooming roses. The sunlight's warmth on her shoulders was soothing and she paused near the rose garden to enjoy the moment. As she gazed into deep blue sky, optimism rose, dispelling her gloomy thoughts. Everything would be all right. *Eventually*.

With renewed vigor, she strode along, choosing the path through the carved animal topiaries. Then her heart gave a painful lurch and she stopped short, heels slipping on the gravel.

Legs and a pair of man's shoes protruded from under the foliage elephant's trunk. *Has someone else been murdered?*

Faith screamed, her hands flying up. Her tote sailed from her grip and landed on the lawn nearby, the contents spilling.

Deb Cabot stepped into view. "Hold on, Faith. It's okay. He's just acting."

The man sat up with a smile. "I guess I'm doing a good job."

"Lie back down, Mark," Deb ordered. "The detectives are coming." He promptly plopped flat and shut his eyes. To Faith she said, "We're playing a game where teams are solving a case." As she spoke, a swarm of guests came into view, carrying magnifying glasses and wielding clipboards. They spotted Mark and moved as a unit toward him.

Faith smiled weakly as she gathered her things from the grass. "I guess I should review the schedule of activities so I'm not surprised again."

"Better yet, join us." Deb threw her a wink and then turned to the group of guests, barking information and orders at them exactly like a camp counselor.

Or a drill sergeant. Faith suppressed a laugh as she continued on her way. Would all the retreats feature such entertaining, hands-on activities? She had pictured guests sitting around, discussing literature while sedately drinking tea.

With the visitors occupied by the game outdoors, the mansion was quiet. Faith unlocked the library door and set the sign to Open, although she doubted anyone would come in until later.

Her gaze fell on the locked cases of the special collection, which held rows of glowing leather volumes, many with titles embossed in gold. Access to such rare and beautiful books was a thrilling treat at any time. Being placed in charge of their care was a professional coup.

I wonder if anything else has been stolen or switched. Being compelled to learn if any besides *A Study in Scarlet* were forgeries was a disconcerting and painful task.

No time like the present. Sighing deeply, Faith pulled out a pair of white gloves and the keys to the cabinets. Next she printed a list from the catalog to check against each book to ensure they matched their descriptions.

After an initial hesitation she became absorbed in her task, enjoying the beauty of each precious book both for its content and the care that went into its printing. Illustrated Bibles, Roman and Greek philosophy, nonfiction works, and classic novels were all part of the special collection.

As she was marveling at the tooled leather covering a 1532 edition of Chaucer— extremely valuable—the library door swung open and Wolfe Jaxon entered. She forced herself to smile, glad he couldn't read her mind—or discern her suspicions.

To her relief, he returned her smile. "Good morning, Faith. What are you up to today?" He nodded at the priceless book she held.

She slid it gently back into place. "I'm familiarizing myself with the special collection. It's incredible."

"It is." He joined her at the bookshelf. "My great-grandfather was a true connoisseur of fine books. He traveled all over Europe building this collection."

And who was responsible for decimating it? Faith studied Wolfe's handsome profile as he gazed at the rows of books.

"My grandfather made me read many of these. He thought they might teach me something, not to mention improving my manners." He pointed to *Meditations* by Marcus Aurelius, a Roman emperor. "This one was tough but I learned a lot."

Faith regarded him with bemusement. "No wonder it was tough. It's in Latin."

Wolfe shrugged. "Learning Greek and Latin was part of the deal.

He also taught me how to handle rare books—with kid gloves, as the expression goes. My friends used to tease me since he made me wear gloves like yours."

"I bet they did." Faith tried to imagine a much younger Wolfe laboring under the tutelage of his stern grandfather. With such a background, would he value ancient books or resent them? It was his mother who founded the retreat, she remembered. His interests seemed to include other pursuits, sailing among them.

Wolfe shrugged. "I had the last laugh when we went to college. I was miles ahead of everyone else."

"Me too. Many of my friends hated studying literature. I loved it." They shared a smile, then, feeling uncomfortable with him watching, Faith decided to continue browsing later. She locked the bookcase and stripped off her gloves. "Was there anything in particular you needed?"

He leaned against the arm of a chair and crossed his arms. "Not really. I wanted to see how you were settling in."

Faith considered how best to answer. Honestly, she decided, since despite the murder, it was the best job she'd ever had. "I really enjoy being here. The library is fantastic, the guests are great, and I adore the cottage. So does Watson."

"But?" He cocked a brow. "I can tell you have reservations. I can hear them in your voice."

Why was he probing? To find out how she felt, or something more devious—what she suspected or knew? Faith tried to brush off the question with a laugh. "Well, things didn't exactly get off on the right foot with Doris Lincoln's death and all . . ."

"That's what I'm worried about." Wolfe left his perch and moved toward her, concern shadowing his eyes. "I really hope this terrible situation won't drive you away." He halted slightly too close for comfort, forcing her to step back, right up against the desk.

Conflicting thoughts swirled in Faith's brain as she stared up into his handsome face. Of course she wanted to keep her job. But at what price? By no fault of her own, she was a prime suspect in a murder case. Even if cleared, she would never be able to relax until the real killer was unmasked and she found out who had switched the Sherlock Holmes first edition with a forgery. If Wolfe Jaxon or some retreat employee was involved, that would change everything.

"I'll stay," she finally said. "As long as it's mutually agreeable."

Wolfe grinned. "Then I hope that means a long, long time." He gave her a brisk nod. "I'll let you get back to work." He turned to go.

"Just a minute, Wolfe. I have something to ask you." Faith steeled herself, knowing her question might destroy their tentative rapport.

"Go ahead, shoot."

"I was wondering . . . that week before Labor Day, did Doris discuss any concerns with you?"

Frowning, he shook his head. "No, I didn't even see her that week. What concerns are you talking about?"

Faith's heart sank. She couldn't bring up the scheduled meeting between Doris and Wolfe since she'd learned about it by prying. Why was he denying it? "No reason, really. I thought maybe she was unhappy about something here at the retreat and . . . and . . ."

"And that's why she was killed?" His voice dripped with skepticism. "Ridiculous. If Doris Lincoln had any issues here, I never heard about them." He glanced at his watch. "Excuse me, Faith, I have a conference call in five minutes." Turning on his heel, he strode out of the room, the stiff set of his shoulders conveying exasperation.

Faith watched him go, misery welling. If Wolfe was innocent, she couldn't risk offending him or she would lose her job. And if he was guilty of book forgery or murder—or both—then it wasn't safe to cross him either.

In her search for the truth, she should tread lightly. Very lightly indeed.

12

With a sigh, Faith went to her desk to check in a stack of returned books. The retreat allowed borrowing as long as guests signed their name and room number. That way any stray volumes could be tracked down before people checked out.

The library door opened again and, half-expecting Wolfe's return, Faith swiveled around in her chair, heart jumping. Benedict Sinclaire entered, followed by Molly, who trotted over to Faith and sniffed her shoes.

"Aren't you playing the detective game, Benedict?" Faith reached down and fondled Molly's silky ears. The little dog appeared to have recovered fully from her upset stomach. Molly licked her hand in response.

Benedict shook his head. "I skipped it. I wasn't feeling very well so I slept in."

Faith noticed his drawn expression and the dark circles under his eyes. "Are you coming down with something?"

He shrugged. "I don't think so. I haven't been sleeping well, that's all." Plucking at his lower lip, he scanned the volumes in the special collection. "I am so envious of Jaxon's Arthur Conan Doyle editions." He reached up one hand, letting it hover near the glass, a yearning look in his eyes.

Faith fished for the keys. "Do you want to take a closer look?"

His eyes brightened. "Would you let me? I'll be careful."

"You'll have to wear these." She tossed him a clean pair of large white gloves.

He drew them on, watching eagerly as she put on her own gloves and unlocked the case. "Sir Arthur only wrote four Sherlock Holmes novels and fifty-six Holmes short stories, you know. Not a very large output, but it's had a huge influence on literature and entertainment."

Faith thought about the dozens of derivative works she'd seen featuring Sherlock Holmes or other characters from Conan Doyle's work. "That's true. Your books are inspired by Sherlock Holmes, aren't they?"

Benedict nodded. "Yes. I write the Doctor Watson mysteries. In my books, Holmes has retired but Watson continues to work with Scotland Yard to solve cases."

"That sounds like an interesting premise."

He smiled modestly. "I've done all right. I've won an Edgar or two." Those were awards bestowed by the Mystery Writers of America for the best books each year.

"Impressive." Faith gestured at the books. "Is there one in particular you want to see?"

"That one." Benedict sighed with pleasure as he pointed to *The Adventures of Sherlock Holmes*, a collection of short stories.

Faith slid the book, which had a pale blue cover, off the shelf and placed it on a nearby table. Benedict took a seat and carefully opened the front cover. "This is the very first edition, printed in 1892. I only have a later one but I hope to upgrade soon." He leafed ahead, gesturing to Faith. "Take a peek at this. It's signed."

She leaned over his shoulder, noticing a faded signature on the title page—*Arthur Conan Doyle*—in old-fashioned British-style script. "Nice."

Benedict reared back, pointing a shaking finger at the signature, his mouth working in distress. "That's not Sir Arthur's signature. It's a fake."

Faith peered more closely, squinting her eyes. "Are you sure? It looks old."

The writer grunted. "Trust me, it isn't real. I've seen dozens of authentic Sir Arthur signatures. I even own one or two." He turned to the publishing information. "The book appears to be a first edition, so someone added the signature to boost the value even higher."

Faith sank into a chair beside Benedict. "So now the first edition is marred by a forged signature."

"That's right." Benedict rubbed his chin as he regarded the forgery. "Old Mr. Jaxon must have been taken in when he bought it."

From all she'd heard, Wolfe's great-grandfather wasn't the type to be hoodwinked. This was another substitution, Faith was sure. Someone had stolen the book with the real signature and replaced it with this one, believing that no one would notice for a long time.

To forestall any gossip, Faith agreed with Benedict. "You're right. What a shame. I'll have to let Wolfe know."

Benedict's grin was wry. "Better you than me." He stripped off his gloves, leaving them in balls on the table. "Thanks for letting me look, even if it was a disappointment." He pushed his chair back and whistled for Molly.

"Anytime." As the duo left the library, Faith replaced the book and locked the case. An odd thought struck: *Had Benedict deliberately asked to see that book, knowing the signature was forged? Had he wanted to bring it to her attention for some reason?*

She turned the key again. This afternoon she would take the book down to Franklin Woodbury's shop. Maybe he could help her sort this all out.

Her cell rang, announcing that her aunt was calling. "Hi, Aunt Eileen. I'm so glad to hear from you."

"Having a bad day?" Eileen always seemed to pick up on Faith's moods.

Faith shrugged. It was beyond bad, actually. "I really can't talk about it over the phone."

"Why don't you come for dinner, then? I was going to do chicken breasts on my grill one more time before I put it away for the winter."

The idea of a meal with her aunt perked Faith up. "Want me to stop at the store for some potato salad?" The local grocery made great food to go. "And I'll swing by the bakery for dessert."

"Perfect. I've got garden vegetables on hand for a green salad."

They arranged a time and Faith hung up with a new attitude. She wasn't in this alone. She had her aunt and her new friends to see her through.

The day fortunately remained quiet thanks to other activities going on, so Faith got a good deal of paperwork done. She also made small tweaks to procedures, attempting to streamline them to make things easier. From what she could gather, other librarians at the retreat had depended upon their memories more than Faith thought was prudent. In addition, she wanted to hire an assistant so she could take time off if necessary. That person would need to be able to find what they needed.

At four thirty, she locked the door and removed *The Adventures of Sherlock Holmes* from the case. This was becoming a bad habit, but she really didn't have a choice, not with a murderer lurking. She wrapped the book and placed it gently in her tote, aware that if by some chance Benedict might be wrong, the volume would be extremely valuable. She'd handle it that way until she knew otherwise.

Her glance fell on one of the public library computers, which she hadn't shut down yet. To deal with Franklin Woodbury, she had the feeling she needed a little more ammunition. His default position appeared to be skepticism—no matter which side you were on.

Signing on to the Internet, she did a search and printed the results, several sample Arthur Conan Doyle signatures. Then she logged off and left, praying this ordeal would soon be resolved.

Lighthouse Bay bustled with people enjoying the sunny autumn afternoon. Walking to the bookstore, Faith dodged small children eating ice cream cones, dog walkers, and a gaggle of teenagers more intent on teasing one another than paying attention to other people trying to get by them.

Up ahead a block or so, she spotted Marlene Russell's familiar figure headed in the same direction. By some fluke, was she going to the bookstore? That would be a disaster. Faith ducked into the entryway of a boutique and watched the manager's neat blonde bun bobbing down the sidewalk.

A clerk appeared in the shop doorway, staring curiously at Faith, who pretended to admire the display of golfing and sailing attire in the window. The tiny whales on the pockets were definitely not her style, she decided. She was hopeless at golf anyway.

When the clerk lost interest, Faith peeked around the corner again, hoping she hadn't lost Marlene. After a minute, she spotted her turning down a side street, the one where the leather store was located. Maybe she was going there.

Giving the manager a minute longer, Faith waited, moving aside to let customers in and out of the boutique. Then she scurried along the row of stores to Franklin's, feeling as though she were living inside a thriller novel. Who knew a trip to a bookstore could be fraught with such peril?

Inside the dim, cool interior of the bookstore, it took Faith's eyes a few minutes to adjust. She spotted Franklin hunkered down behind a bookshelf, arranging books. He straightened with a groan, holding one hand to his back. "How may I help you, Miss Newberry?" His tone seemed to say, "Make it quick."

Faith steeled herself, resisting the bookseller's intimidating, impatient manner. "I have another book for you to look at."

He limped his way behind the counter, straightening his eyeglasses as he went. "Where did you find this one?"

"I'd rather not say." Faith set her tote down and carefully pulled out the book. After setting it on the glass, she unwrapped it for his inspection.

Franklin inspected the book's cover first, humming under his breath. Next he leafed through to the title page. "Ah. Signed. Nice, very nice indeed."

Faith sucked in a breath. "It might be nice, except . . ." She pulled out the printed signatures. "I think the signature is a fake." She laid them beside the one in the book so he could compare.

The bookseller's eyes darted back and forth between the book and the pages. Then he shook his head. "I don't see a problem here." Taking off his glasses, he rubbed the bridge of his nose. "This seems to be a pattern, Miss Newberry. You finding problems with books."

His unfair and unkind remark stung like a slap in the face. And as if she had been struck, Faith's cheeks heated up. "That's because there are problems," she said indignantly. "I don't want to find them, they're forced on me."

A smirk flitted over his face. "Is that so?" He stabbed a finger at the book. "In this case, I think you're overreacting. There are often variations in signatures, and it takes more than a glance to verify authenticity."

"So it could be authentic then." Faith paused to let that sink in, then said, "And what about *A Study in Scarlet*? That was definitely a forgery. Did you have any luck in finding out if an original was sold recently?"

Franklin began to fuss with items on the countertop. "I'm afraid not. I've searched nationwide and haven't turned up a thing."

Faith was stumped. She began to wrap up *The Adventures of Sherlock Holmes*. Maybe Mr. Jaxon had been fooled and purchased a *Scarlet* forgery decades ago. Or the switch had been made a long time ago and there was no way to trace it now.

"I'll be on my way then," she said, picking up her bag. "Have a good night."

Lost in thought, Faith didn't see Marlene Russell until she was almost on top of her. "Hello, Faith. Doing a little shopping in your downtime?" Marlene's eyes darted between Faith's face and the tote she was clutching. "I saw you come out of the bookstore."

Uh-oh, I'm in trouble now. Faith thought quickly. "Oh yes. I bought a book on cat diseases." At Marlene's sour expression, she quickly added, "Not that Watson isn't in perfect health, but I always think it's important to be prepared."

Marlene snorted. "I'd rather see the resort be an animal-free zone, but Mrs. Jaxon won't have it any other way."

Thank goodness for Wolfe's mother. "Pets provide a lot of comfort," Faith said. "Help the sick and elderly feel better and all that."

Marlene took a step back, a look of horror on her face. "You're not . . . ill, are you?"

Faith forced a laugh. "Of course not. I was speaking hypothetically. I'm perfectly healthy." She waved the tote. "Well, I won't take up any more of your time . . ."

As she hoped, the manager took the cue. "I'll see you later." Then she turned back. "Oh yes, there's a scavenger hunt tomorrow night after dinner, and I'd like you to take part."

A scavenger hunt wasn't exactly Faith's cup of tea but she nodded. "All right. As long as it doesn't interfere with my library duties."

Marlene raised her brows. "They're not too taxing, are they? We could always cut your hours."

A thrill of alarm ran down Faith's spine. On top of being a murder suspect and skulking around investigating forgeries, her job was in jeopardy? "No no. Everything is great. Really. I love it. I love everything about it." She bit her lip, certain she sounded like a babbling fool.

Marlene shot her one last glare. "Glad to hear it." She stomped away down the sidewalk.

Faith went in the other direction, eager to get out of downtown before she ran into someone else. After stopping at the bakery for fudgy brownies, she swung into the grocery store for a tub of potato salad.

Eileen lived on a street lined with quaint homes built in the early part of the twentieth century. Faith thought her house, a classic Craftsman bungalow with brown shingle siding and a wide front porch supported by stone pillars, was adorable. As she pulled in behind Eileen's sporty ruby-red Mustang, she took a moment to admire the cottage-style flower gardens, still pretty even this late in the year. In addition to her passion for books—especially mysteries—Eileen loved gardening and was an active member of the garden club.

Faith grabbed the bakery box and grocery bag from the front seat and slid out of the car. Then she paused. She really should stow her tote with its precious cargo out of sight. Laughing at her paranoia, she set the food down on the seat and carried her bag to the rear of the car. Although the CRV didn't have a real trunk, it did have a screen that covered items placed back there.

She tucked the tote inside and draped a beach blanket over it for good measure. That should keep it out of view from prying eyes.

Faith walked around to the back of the house, where Eileen was grilling chicken breasts on the back patio. "We'll eat on the porch since it's such a nice evening," her aunt said after greeting her with a one-armed hug. "Set your things in there." She pointed to the screened enclosure overlooking the spacious backyard. "Oh, and pour yourself a glass of iced tea or coffee. I made both."

After pouring a glass of frosty iced tea, Faith joined her aunt outside. While waiting for the chicken to cook, they sat on lounge chairs next to the heated in-ground pool.

Faith leaned back and gazed up at the trees overhead, feeling the tension drain out of her limbs. "I love it back here."

"Me too," Eileen said. "Even though the pool's a lot of work, I really enjoy having it." She stretched her fingers out with a grimace. "Plus it helps my arthritis." A rheumatoid arthritis sufferer, Eileen did her best not to let the crippling disease slow her down.

"How are you doing?" Faith asked tentatively. Eileen rarely spoke about her illness, which fortunately had periods of remission.

Eileen rubbed her knuckles. "Not bad lately. The new medication is working well." She smiled at her niece. "But enough about me. What's going on?"

"I barely know where to begin. Murder investigation or forgery?"

"My goodness, you do lead an exciting life, just like a mystery novel." Eileen raised her chair a notch, signaling her intent interest.

Faith chuckled. "That's what I was thinking earlier. I felt like I was in a spy movie when I was sneaking another book down to Franklin's shop."

"I can't wait to hear about that. But tell me, what's new with the murder investigation? I noticed it made the news."

"I know. I saw some articles on the Internet. Fortunately I wasn't mentioned." Faith frowned. "You don't think Mom and Dad will hear about it, do you?" She pictured their worry if they learned of the murder while too far away to help. Her father would be especially upset. As a retired police sergeant, he would want to make sure Faith was treated fairly. He'd probably wade right into the middle of the investigation.

Eileen shook her head. "I doubt the news will travel that far. When I was in Italy, you barely caught any American news unless it was very high profile, involving the president or something. And since you have to buy international cell phone access there, you're really out of touch."

"Mom and Dad decided not to do that, remember? They wanted to really get away." At the time Faith had been slightly hurt since she was used to easy access to her parents. Now she was grateful. "Anyway, the big news is, they found the murder weapon." She paused. "The fireplace poker from the cottage. Remember it was missing?"

Eileen jerked in surprise, splashing her tea on the patio. "She was killed at the cottage? I thought it happened in the mansion."

"Me too. I think it was in the garden, actually, since they didn't find any evidence inside the cottage." Faith's lips twisted. "I was banned for a day while they searched. I'm so glad they didn't find evidence in there. I would have been homeless until they released the scene."

Eileen reached out and patted Faith's knee. "You can always stay here, remember that."

"That's good to know. Anyway, let me tell you what else I've learned." Faith filled her in about mentioning Doris's belongings to the police, the confiscation of the mansion plans during the search, and the discovery that Doris had a contentious relationship with Sandra Baker, the conference organizer. "Doris also didn't get along with Laura, one of the maids whom she tried to get fired, and she planned a meeting with Wolfe Jaxon before she died but they never met, according to him. I bet she was going to tell him about the forged book."

"Wow. Let me absorb all that for a minute." Her head whipped around as smoke starting pouring from the grill. "Uh-oh. I'd better get that chicken off." She jumped up from the chair and darted over to the grill. As she grabbed the tongs and lifted the lid, she grinned at Faith. "I guess I am feeling pretty good, to move that fast."

The chicken was fine and after Eileen transferred it to a platter, they moved onto the porch. By common consent, their discussion was tabled while they ate. Faith forced herself to forget everything and savor juicy herbed chicken, creamy potato salad, crisp greens, and best of all, brownies so fudgy they were almost black.

"This brownie is so good." Faith broke off another piece and popped it into her mouth. "I'm stuffed but I can't stop eating." She sipped decaf coffee to wash it down. The combination of flavors was divine.

Eileen laughed. "I know what you mean." She'd made quite a dent in her own dessert. "I have to ration my visits to Snickerdoodles."

Faith patted her full stomach. "Between the bakery and the wonderful retreat meals, I'll have to watch my waistline like a hawk."

"Another cup of coffee?" Eileen reached for Faith's cup.

"Thanks. I'm glad it's decaf. I have had enough trouble sleeping already."

"We can't have that." Eileen went into the kitchen for a moment for refills.

Faith studied the twilight garden, watching the shadows deepen under the trees. Much as she loved the cottage and the retreat, it was good to get away for a little while and gain some perspective.

"So is there anything else you want to tell me?" Eileen asked as she placed the coffee cups on the table. "Or did we cover everything?"

"Actually there is. But I'm not quite sure if it has a bearing on the murder." Faith added a little cream to her coffee and stirred. "I found another problem book. This one has an author signature that might be fake. Apparently people forge author signatures to raise the value of first editions."

Eileen's eyes widened. "Really? That's awful." As a fellow librarian and book lover, she shared Faith's commitment to the care and keeping of books.

Faith told her about Benedict's claim the signature was a forgery and Franklin's refusal to make that judgment.

"Maybe he's right. Benedict isn't a book appraiser, is he?"

"No, but he has studied Arthur Conan Doyle's work extensively. Probably much more than Franklin has. After all, Franklin deals in books written by many authors and he can't be an expert on all of them."

"Good point." Lost in thought, Eileen stared out into the garden. The night was almost upon them now and stars were twinkling above the trees. "Maybe you should get a second opinion. I thought Franklin was an expert, but I'm not impressed with his response in this case."

"Me neither. I had to tell him *A Study in Scarlet* was fake." Faith drained her cup. "I'll look for someone else in Boston tomorrow."

"It's disconcerting that the special collection has been tampered with," Eileen said. "I can't believe Wolfe's great-grandfather was so easily fooled as to buy worthless books."

Before Faith could reply, a shrieking sound shattered the still evening. Faith leaped to her feet. "That's my car alarm!"

13

"Are you sure?" Eileen asked. "I've heard other alarms go off in the neighborhood."

"Believe me, it is. I recognize that horrible sound." Faith dug in her purse for her keys and ran for the porch door. What could have set off the alarm? It was touchy sometimes, and to her chagrin and the annoyance of strangers, she'd had to hurry to turn it off. If it hadn't been for the valuable book in the back, she probably wouldn't have locked her car in Eileen's drive. It was generally a very safe neighborhood.

As she skirted the house, she saw a figure sprinting down the driveway. A nearby streetlight's glow was too dim to allow her to gauge anything but a general sense of height and weight, both medium. The person was carrying something tucked under an arm. The book from Castleton?

A wave of fear and anger swept over her. "Hey you!" she yelled. "Stop right now."

Of course the person didn't obey. Instead he or she stepped up the pace. Heart pounding, Faith reached her car. At a glance she saw the rear side window was broken and the door was hanging open. She pressed the fob to stop the terrible squawking of the alarm and then dashed around back to open the hatch.

Reaching into the hatchback, Faith shoved the blanket aside. When she saw the tote was still there, her relief was so overwhelming that she swayed, closing her eyes for a second. Then she tugged the bag open and confirmed that, yes, the book was inside.

Had she imagined that the person was carrying something? What else could possibly be missing? Faith moved around to the side of the car and leaned through the open passenger door to check the backseat.

Glass sparkled on every surface but otherwise the space was empty.

Eileen appeared by her side, gasping at the broken window. "Did they take anything?"

Faith bent over, hands on her thighs, gasping for air as she began to laugh. She collapsed against the side of the car, roaring, tears streaming.

"Faith. Faith." Her aunt shook her arm. "What's going on?"

"He . . . he stole . . . a plastic bag full of trash," she managed to get out. "Can you believe it? All that effort for worthless junk." A sturdy bag from a conference had contained an old binder full of outdated notes and other random bits and pieces she'd stuffed inside. Was it only coincidence that it was about the same shape and size as the tote containing the rare book?

"I'm glad nothing important is missing, but I'm calling the police anyway." Eileen pulled out her cell phone and punched in the number.

The police arrived within minutes, the blue and white strobing lights flickering in the treetops. When the driver door opened and an officer emerged, Faith recognized Officer Tobin. His eyes widened when he saw Faith sitting beside her aunt on the front porch steps, the yard now well lit by porch and accent lights.

As he approached, his gaze fell on Faith's car and he stopped to examine the open door with its broken window. Faith and Eileen joined him.

"Good evening, Mrs. Piper. Miss Newberry." Resting his hands on his hips, he gave each of them an appraising glance. "Take me through what happened."

Faith explained how they'd heard the alarm while eating and had arrived in front of the house in time to see someone run off.

Tobin took notes on his phone. "Anything missing?"

"A bag of trash." At her own deadpan words, Faith had to suppress a snort of laughter. Eileen giggled.

Tobin cocked a brow. "What is so amusing?"

"I'm sorry, Officer. I was so upset to have my car broken into and then the only thing missing was a bag of garbage from the backseat. Isn't that strange?"

"Okay." The officer drew out the word but dutifully made the note. "Any idea why someone would do such a thing?"

Faith hesitated. If she mentioned carrying around something valuable belonging to the Jaxons, without their knowledge no less, it would open up a whole can of worms.

"Not really," she finally said. "But I don't know the minds of thieves as well as you do."

Her answer stumped him for moment. He cleared his throat. "Well, we have had a few smash-and-grabs around town. Perhaps it was one of those."

Faith hoped so too. At least her instinct about stowing the tote had been a good one. "Can I get a copy of your police report? I'll need to file a claim with my insurance company so I can get the window replaced."

After Tobin left, Eileen helped her vacuum up the glass and tape cardboard over the broken window.

"Be careful, Faith," Eileen said to Faith as she prepared to leave. "I think you're treading into dangerous territory."

"You're probably right." Faith gave her aunt an impulsive hug. "But I can't see any way out but forward until I get some answers. Otherwise I'm the perfect scapegoat." *And some people think being a librarian is boring!*

The cat's ears perked up. What was that sound? He glanced at his person, who was still sleeping, curled in the ball that made such a nice nest for him.

The noise came again, faint but easily detectable by a cat with superior hearing. He jumped down from the bed and ran down the stairs, "on little cat feet," as the poet said.

At the front door he sniffed at the crack on the bottom. As a result, the snuffling on the other side increased to a whine, an eerie moan of distress.

He gave an inquisitive mew, sympathetic despite the natural friction between species. The door banged as the creature threw itself against it, and the whining spiraled into a howl.

Footsteps thumped on the second floor. Good, his person was coming to provide comfort. She did that so well.

A piercing howl cut through Faith's slumber, sending her up and out of bed before she understood what was happening. Her first thought was Watson, who was nowhere to be found, but his howl was more of a yowl.

The unearthly sound came again as Faith staggered to the stairs and made her way down. She saw Watson, his nose pressed up against the crack at the bottom of the front door. "Who is making that racket?" she asked him as she flipped on the porch light and unlocked the front door. Now she recognized the wail as a dog in distress. Was the poor thing hurt, maybe hit by a car?

She pulled the door open. Molly lay huddled on the small porch, head tilted to produce another howl. "Molly, Molly. What's the matter, girl?" Faith hunkered down and stroked the little dog's head. In response, she nestled close to Faith, practically crawling into her lap. Faith gently ran her hands over the dog's trunk, her legs, and head, but could find no injury.

Faith heard the crunching of footsteps and a second later, Benedict trudged into view. "There you are, girl. I was wondering where you ran off to."

Molly perked up, struggling in Faith's arms. She let her go and Molly ran to her master, who gathered her in his arms.

"She was howling at my door," Faith said. "But she doesn't seem to be hurt, thank goodness."

Benedict buried his nose in Molly's fur. "That's a relief. We were taking a late-night stroll when she got away from me."

Late-night indeed. When Faith glanced at the bedside clock, she'd seen it was barely two o'clock. Although she longed for her bed, she asked impulsively, "Would you like to come in and warm up? It's chilly out here." The little dog was shivering, whether from shock, cold, or excitement, she couldn't tell.

The author paused, then said, "All right. I owe you an explanation anyway."

Faith led the way to the living room, where she began to build a fire, watched closely by Watson, who supervised. "Have a seat. Shall I make some hot chocolate?" When Molly's ears perked up, she laughed. "Not for you, girl."

Benedict collapsed into an armchair, still holding his dog. "That sounds nice. If it's not too much trouble."

As if getting up in the middle of the night wasn't trouble enough! Faith was eager to hear his explanation and wondered what he was referring to. Doris Lincoln? The book with the fake signature? Something else?

She was getting good at making fires in this fireplace and soon flames were crackling, sending dancing shadows over the walls and ceiling. Benedict and Molly both sighed, snuggling even deeper into the armchair. Watson curled up on the hearthrug, one eye on the visitors.

Faith rose to her feet. "I'll be right back." Another set of sighs was the only reply. In the kitchen, she made hot chocolate at record speed, at the last moment adding a few oatmeal raisin cookies on a plate.

She set everything on a tray and when she entered the living room, she saw that both dog and cat were snoring. Benedict, on the other hand, was weeping silently, shoulders shaking. Tears ran down his face, gleaming trails in the firelight.

"Oh my." Faith set the tray down and grabbed a box of tissues. She brought them over and set them on the chair's arm. "What's wrong, Benedict?"

Not wanting to embarrass him further by staring, she picked up her hot chocolate and gazed into the fire while he blew his nose and wiped his eyes.

"I'm sorry," he choked out. "I wasn't planning on breaking down like that."

"No one ever plans to break down," Faith said. "It just happens." She remembered a meltdown or two when her relationship with her boyfriend John Schultz was falling apart. She was well over that now but definitely could sympathize with overwhelming emotions.

"There are so many memories for me in this house." Benedict's voice was soft. "Molly and I had good times here, didn't we, girl?" Waking up, Molly licked his nose in response.

Faith took his words as an opening. "I gather you knew Doris quite well."

Benedict chuckled softly. "Oh, you could say that. We were in love."

Although half-expecting it, this reversal of his earlier denials regarding Doris made Faith's head spin. She sipped her cocoa, hoping he would continue to confide in her. She also mentally located her cell phone and the number of steps to the closest door, in case he had more to confess than affection for the dead librarian.

"Or at least *I* was. I may have jumped the gun a bit with my declarations. It had been so long since I'd felt that way about a woman."

Faith's tension rose. Unrequited love was often a motive for murder, she'd gathered from books and, yes, real life.

"She was beautiful, kind, intelligent, and oh, so spunky." Benedict's face was dreamy as he stared into the fire, as though seeing Doris imprinted on the flames. "She always stood up for what she believed in and I admired that. So many people today are wimps."

"I understand Doris was quite spunky," Faith said, taking the opportunity to see what she could learn about her predecessor. "Didn't she challenge her old boss about the library budget?"

He cocked a brow. "You heard about that? Yes, Doris took on Sandra and the system." He chuckled again. "And she won. The branches are getting more adequate budgets now, thanks to her."

"That is commendable." Faith injected a note of admiration into her voice. "How was she getting on here at Castleton?"

Benedict frowned. "Not that well, frankly. Oh, she was excited to get the position—Who wouldn't be? It's a dream job—but it fell apart pretty quickly."

"I'm sorry to hear that." Faith was sincere. "Do you know what went wrong? Maybe it will help me navigate the situation."

He stroked his chin thoughtfully. "She didn't give me any details, I'm afraid. But I do know she was beside herself with anxiety."

"Was she going to leave the retreat?" Faith held her breath, hoping to fill in that part of the mystery.

"She talked about it, but I'm not sure what she decided." He gulped, tears brimming in his eyes again. "She stopped confiding in me."

Maybe Doris wanted to protect him—or maybe she didn't trust him. Faith groaned inwardly with frustration. She still didn't know enough about the situation. "When did you see her last? If you feel like you can talk about it, that is."

"The weekend before Labor Day. I came over that Friday night, excited to spend a weekend with her without the manager and everyone else breathing down our necks."

"I hear you," Faith said, hoping to inject a lighter note. "I'm still getting used to that myself."

He began to stroke Molly's back over and over, a repetitive motion. "Everything was fine until she told me she wanted to cool things off." His tone was bitter. "And here I thought we were getting closer. I had even checked out rings. Silly me."

Oh my. Faith could relate. Her boyfriend had also given her the "I need space" speech. It had felt like a slap in the face. She pictured the scene, the pair in the cottage, Doris telling him she wanted to break up—what happened next? Faith's midsection tensed as her body went on high alert. As if sensing her shift in mood, Watson opened one eye.

Benedict bowed his head, his face miserable. "I feel so guilty."

14

Faith's chest tightened. Was she about to hear a confession of murder? Once again she mentally reviewed her surroundings.

He was silent for a long moment, so long that Faith finally asked, careful not to sound accusing, "What do you mean, you feel guilty?"

Benedict scrubbed a hand over his face. "Things got out of hand. I was angry and I lost my patience. I'd been so careful to that point to give her room, not to pressure her. But then I blew it."

Faith scooted to the edge of her chair and Watson sat up straight, tail twitching. "So you got into an argument?" She pictured the scene, Benedict grabbing the poker, striking Doris . . . but the police said it hadn't happened in this room.

His laugh was hollow. "I'll say. We had a good old-fashioned screaming match. Good thing everyone else was away—well, almost everyone. I accused her of leading me on, of using me . . . I helped her when she was between jobs . . . the whole bit. Threw it all in her face."

"It happens to the best of us." Faith's knee began to hammer up and down. She stopped it by pressing down with her fist. "I've chewed out a few people myself."

"I bet they didn't die afterward."

Another silence, broken only by a thump and crackle as a log settled in the fireplace. Faith and Watson jumped. Faith cleared her throat. "That must have been awful."

He gave a sob. "It was. And still is. I'll never forgive myself. I stormed out of here in the middle of the night and drove away."

Before or after Doris died? Faith's mind buzzed, seeking a way to ask. "How did Doris take it?"

"She didn't want me to leave. But I did anyway."

If Benedict was telling the truth, then he didn't kill her. Relief swamped Faith and she collapsed back into her chair. Watson gave a yawn and curled into a ball, his bobbed tail touching his nose.

Benedict wiped his eyes with a tissue and blew his nose. "I have to live with it the rest of my life. My last words to someone I loved were cruel and angry."

"You didn't speak to her again?" Maybe she could narrow the time of death.

He looked sheepish. "I got a text around 8 a.m. the next morning but I didn't answer it. Another lost opportunity."

"So she died after that. On Sunday, not Saturday." Realizing she'd spoken out loud, Faith clapped a hand over her mouth. This new information didn't clear her entirely since she had been alone for hours at Eileen's on Sunday. But at least she could prove her drive past the retreat on Saturday was innocent.

Benedict's mouth dropped open in horror. "You mean I might have been able to prevent her death? Oh no. Why didn't I think of that before?" He scrambled to his feet, clutching at Molly. "I've got to go."

Faith held out a hand. "Wait, Benedict. If you had stayed with Doris, maybe you would be dead now too."

"Don't try to placate me." He shook his head violently as he scrambled toward the door. "I can't believe how self-absorbed I've been. I'm a horrible person." He fumbled at the doorknob and then he was gone, fleeing into the night.

Faith sank back into the chair. "Well, Watson, I think I blew it."

Watson blinked his eyes, as if in agreement. Faith picked him up and together they returned to the sanctum of her bedroom.

The next morning, a groggy Faith arrived at the manor to find the Main Hall swarming with chattering, milling guests. Rows of chairs had been set up for a lecture but the podium was deserted. Faith edged by the refreshment table, hoping to grab a coffee before sliding through to the sanctuary of the library.

"Try one of those chocolate croissants," Brooke said. "They're divine."

Faith looked up from adding cream to her coffee. "Did you make them?"

Brooke nodded proudly. "Sure did. The strawberry ones too." She straightened the tiered platters. "They're going fast, so hurry." Other offerings included tiny muffins and bagels with cream cheese.

Faith set her coffee down and used tongs to choose a couple of the mini-croissants. *At that size, it didn't count if you ate two, right?* "What's going on?" she asked idly. "I didn't check the schedule."

"Benedict Sinclaire is giving a talk about historical research for novels." Brooke craned her neck, searching the room. "But he still hasn't shown up."

Faith almost dropped her plate in shock. Had the author harmed himself out of remorse over Doris Lincoln's death? Her lips trembled when she asked, "Is he all right?"

Brooke shrugged. "I don't know what's going on." Her eyes widened. "Uh-oh. Here comes Marlene, and it looks like she's got a bee in her bonnet."

Faith turned to see Marlene forcing her way through the crowd, glittering green eyes intent on her target. The target, she realized with a sinking feeling, was her.

"Faith." Marlene's manner was abrupt as always. "I need you to present this morning. We lost our speaker."

Faith's belly lurched. It was worse than she imagined. "Is he . . . dead?"

Marlene's mouth dropped open. "Dead? What are you going

on about now? Benedict isn't feeling well so I thought you could substitute."

She was so relieved at learning Benedict was still among the living that she didn't protest when Marlene handed her the outline for the speech. "The websites are all loaded up on the laptop." Marlene pointed to the podium. "You can handle that, right?"

Faith studied the sheet, which listed the Library of Congress, a newspaper repository at Cornell, and the National Archives in Britain, among others. "You want me to explain what's available at each site for writers to use?"

"That's what I said." Marlene glanced at her watch. "You're on in five."

Feeling as though she should have asked for combat pay, Faith spent the next two hours fielding questions lobbed like missiles from eager researchers, readers, and writers. What a difference from a typical audience, which would have been snoring after she demonstrated the Library of Congress search function. These attendees were eager to apply knowledge and deepened understanding to their passion, the world of Sherlock Holmes.

The event ended up going until lunch, so Faith grabbed a sandwich, covertly replaced the Conan Doyle book that was burning a hole in her tote, and locked up again. No afternoon hours today, although Marlene reminded her to be there at five for the dinner and scavenger hunt.

Her first stop was the town library. "Good afternoon." A full-figured woman with auburn hair stood behind the desk. "Welcome to the Candle House Library."

"Where's Eileen?" The words popped out of Faith's mouth before she could hold them back.

The woman laughed. "That's what they all want to know. I'm Gail Nutter. I work here part-time. Eileen is off today."

Faith approached the desk. "I'm sorry, I didn't mean to be rude." She held out her hand. "I'm Faith Newberry, Eileen's niece."

Gail shook her hand firmly, her hazel eyes glinting with merriment. "I've heard so much about you. You're the librarian up at the big house, right?"

"Yes, I run the Castleton Manor library."

The other librarian clasped both hands and rolled her eyes in mock ecstasy. "What wouldn't I give to work there? I heard the collection is spectacular."

Most of it, anyway. "Yes, it is pretty amazing." Faith began to unbutton her coat. "I was hoping to do a little research in the archives. Are they available?"

Gail pointed to the doorway. "Right up those stairs. Door's unlocked."

"Thanks." Faith hung up her coat and picked up her bag.

"What are you researching?" At Faith's glance, Gail raised one hand. "Not being nosy. I thought I might be able to help. I've worked on a number of local historical research projects."

"I'm looking into my ancestor, Josiah Newberry. Have you heard of him?"

"I certainly have. He's the one who died under mysterious circumstances on Captain Angus Jaxon's boat." She raised her brows. "And now you're working for the Jaxons."

Faith laughed. "We Newberrys don't hold a grudge even though our fortunes plummeted after Josiah's death. I'd like to know more about what happened. The story I heard from my relatives is sketchy at best."

"What do you expect after two hundred years, right? I'd check the microfilm of town property records. They include deeds, mortgages, and foreclosures."

Faith trudged up the creaky narrow stairs to the second floor, remembering the creepy visitor from last time. Hopefully no one would dare to bother her in daylight. In the second drawer down, she found the property records for Lighthouse Bay, all the way back to 1704. She checked the index to select the right reels for her family name, both as grantee and grantor.

Although Faith didn't like using microfilm, she was grateful for the indexing, which made her search through the old documents much easier. Handwritten in ornate script, they were extremely hard to read.

She was able to get the gist and soon a sad story emerged. Earlier in the century, Josiah Newberry accumulated many pieces of property, including land, houses, and commercial buildings. At times, Angus Jaxon was a co-owner or mortgage holder. Then, after Josiah's death, there was a trickle, then a flood of sales and foreclosures to satisfy debts. Either they weren't good at managing the estate or Josiah had built a house of cards. In any case, Angus Jaxon was the clear winner, since he ended up with most of the Newberry property. Today the Jaxons were millionaires and the Newberrys were solidly middle-class. If Josiah hadn't died, would the situation be reversed? Or at least equal?

Faith suppressed a pang of envy. She was content with her life and knew that riches didn't create or guarantee happiness. But still, she could understand her ancestors' resentment if Angus Jaxon profited from Josiah's death. The question was, had Josiah really died of an illness, or had he been murdered?

After packing up copies of documents and notes, Faith left the library and walked over to Snickerdoodles Bakery for a snack. Midafternoon, the place was quiet.

"What can I get you?" Jane's smile was friendly as she waited on Faith. "I recommend the caramel mascarpone mini éclairs." She pointed to the treats. "They're from a new recipe straight from Paris."

Faith laughed. "How can I resist? I'll take two and a cup of coffee, please. For here." She lowered her voice to a whisper. "Excuse my ignorance, but what is mascarpone?"

"It's a soft cream cheese." Jane winked. "Very low calorie."

"I'll bet." As Jane selected pastries from the case, Faith said, "The brownies I bought yesterday were scrumptious."

"I'm glad you liked them." Jane set a small plate on the counter and turned to pour Faith a cup of coffee. "I'll have to give you a frequent shopper card. You get free coffee and cookies."

"Definitely. I'll fill it up in a week."

Jane set the cup on the counter and rang up the sale. As Faith swiped her card, the baker asked, "How's it going up at Castleton?"

"Great, just great." Faith punched keys on the pad. "We've got a very interesting group up there this week. Sherlock Holmes fans."

The printer zipped out a receipt and Jane tore it off and handed it to Faith. "Think they'll be able to solve the real-life mystery of what happened to Doris?"

"Somebody needs to." Faith hoped Jane wouldn't bring up the supposed animosity between the Newberrys and the Jaxons again. She tried to forestall the possibility. "Did you know Doris? I'm learning a lot about her. I think we might even have become friends." There. Spread that around.

Jane leaned on the counter, arms crossed. "Doris was a regular customer. She liked to come down here during her time off. She'd sit in that corner"—Jane pointed—"and work on her laptop and drink coffee. She loved the retreat but she liked to get away too."

"I can understand that," Faith said. "Living where you work is pretty intense. But I love it too." Picking up her cup, she moved to the cream and sugar station.

"That's good to hear." Jane opened the bakery case and began to rearrange cookies on a plate.

"I feel really lucky to have my aunt here in town. With her book club, I have ready-made friends. Doris probably didn't have time to become part of the community, did she?"

As she hoped, Jane took the bait. "You're right. She was mostly in here by herself, although she did come in with a couple of people. She

was seeing that writer Benedict Sinclaire and they seemed real happy."
She shook her head. "Tragic." Jane's propensity for gossip asserted itself
again. "But she wasn't so happy with Franklin Woodbury. But who
could blame her? That man would irritate a saint."

"I've met him," Faith said, keeping her voice neutral. "Quite a
respected book dealer, right?"

Jane rolled her eyes. "Maybe so. Doris didn't respect him too much.
They had one of those whisper fights in here. I think Doris won 'cause
Franklin stormed out and hasn't been back since." She sniffed. "Not
that I miss him. He's stingy *and* picky. A bad combination."

"That's for sure." She paused. "Was Doris dating Franklin too? She
seemed to have an active romantic life." Faith laughed. "More active
than mine, that's for sure."

"I have no idea. I only saw them in here once."

Faith picked up her éclairs. "Nice chatting with you. I'd better eat
these though. I have a bunch of errands to run before four."

"Enjoy." Jane turned to her work.

Faith sat at the same table Doris favored, which was privately
situated but had a nice view of the entire bakery and, through a window,
Main Street. From here she could keep an eye on everything going on.

The fact Doris had known Franklin wasn't surprising due to
their respective professions, Faith mused as she took a bite of creamy,
rich éclair. But meeting for coffee and arguing—that was interesting.
Personal or business, that was the question.

Faith's next stop was Donatello's, the leather shop. As she had
the first time, she paused to admire the boots and handbags in the
window. If she survived this murder investigation, she decided, she'd
buy herself a pair of shoe boots. They looked good with skirts as well
as pants, especially with leggings.

The door jingled as she entered the tiny shop. The front was
crammed with shelves and stands holding finished goods, while a rear
workshop was visible through a large open window. The woman Faith

had seen on the last visit and a man were working back there.

The woman glanced up with a warm smile. "Good afternoon."

"Good afternoon to you too. I told you I'd be back."

"I remember." The woman came through the pass-through. "Is there anything special I can help you with today?"

"Actually a friend recommended you and I thought I would see what you had for shoe boots."

"Right this way." The storekeeper led Faith to the shoe area of the store, placed against one wall. "Have a seat and we'll fit you."

Faith perched on the chair and pushed off her pumps. This was moving a little faster than she planned but she decided to go with the flow.

"Who is your friend? I'd like to thank him or her for the referral."

"Doris Lincoln." Faith made a sad face. "Unfortunately she—"

"I know." A dark shadow passed over the woman's pretty face. "She was murdered." The shadow lifted slightly. "How did you know Doris?"

"We're both librarians. Actually, I replaced Doris at Castleton Manor."

"Oh yes. I heard there was a new librarian. Faith Newberry, right?"

"That's right. Nice to meet you." Faith held out her hand.

The woman shook it. "I'm Lucille Donatello and that old man in the back is my husband, Frank." She shot him a teasing glance.

"Be careful what you say, woman." Frank held up two meaty hands. "You'd be lost without my talent." He laughed. "Glad to meet you, Faith."

"Nice to meet you too." Faith gazed around in admiration. "Everything in here is beautiful. I want one of each."

Lucille laughed. "I love a customer with enthusiasm. Frank trained in Florence in one of the best leather workshops. Isn't that right, Frank?"

"Whatever you say, *mia cara*." He sounded preoccupied, and a minute later a sewing machine whirred.

Head cocked, chin resting on one hand, Lucille studied Faith from head to toe. Then she turned to the shelf and held up three different shoe boots for Faith's approval. "You are slender everywhere, including your feet, which are incredibly dainty. So you need a boot that isn't too clunky."

Faith regarded her feet with new appreciation. If a shoemaker complimented them, they must be attractive.

Lucille pulled up a stool and a foot-sizing device. Humming under her breath, she measured the length and width of Faith's feet and then pulled out the right boxes.

"These are premade," she said, "but we can also do custom work." Her glance at Faith was sweet but sly. "Doris often ordered custom shoes and bags."

"That's nice to know," Faith said. "I'm not sure my budget can stretch to that yet." She held out her foot for Lucille.

Lucille slid the boot onto Faith's foot. "Ah, you never know. It's surprisingly affordable." She slipped the other boot on Faith and then urged her to stand. "Walk around."

Faith obeyed. The boots fit beautifully. She paused to admire her feet in a floor mirror. They looked fantastic too. Her heart beat a little faster. Could she, should she?

Why not? "I'll take them."

Lucille laughed. "Seriously? We have two more pairs to try on."

"I don't need to. I know I want these." Faith sat in the seat.

"That's what we like, a lady who knows her mind." Lucille assisted Faith in removing the boots. She set them neatly in their box and then fussed with the tissue. Finally she looked up at Faith. "I am going to say something, but you must keep it in strict confidence, please."

"Of course I will." Was Lucille sharing shoemaking secrets, perhaps?

"Before Doris . . . died, she said things weren't right up at Castleton." Shaking her head, she pressed her lips together. "You must be careful."

Faith's pulse jumped. "What do you mean?"

Lucille glanced at the back room and lowered her voice to a whisper.

"My husband won't like me saying this but I feel I must." She paused. "I'm not convinced that the danger died with Doris."

15

You must be careful. Lucille's words echoed in Faith's mind as she drove back to Castleton Manor. She had been so preoccupied with finding out who killed Doris and getting herself off the hook that she hadn't really considered that she might be in danger too. She shivered, thinking of her strange experiences in the library and the garden. Had the watcher been intent on harming her? Or was it merely someone keeping tabs on her movements?

The best way out is always through. The quote from a Robert Frost poem came to mind. Events were already in motion and all she could do was forge ahead, no matter how blindly. *Help me*, she prayed silently. *I need wisdom.*

After stopping at the cottage to freshen up, drop off her bag and new boots, and, most importantly, feed Watson, Faith headed over to the mansion. The desk clerk directed her to the banquet hall, where she stepped into a scene of managed mayhem.

"Name, please?" the table attendant near the door asked.

"Faith Newberry." She scanned the table, finding her own name tag with the numeral "1" written underneath. She peeled off the backing and pressed it onto her jacket lapel. "What does the number mean?"

The woman checked her name off. "That's your table and scavenger hunt team. Dinner is a buffet and there's also a beverage station."

Now the noise and chaos made sense. Guests were lining up at the food and drink tables and then finding their seats. As Faith crossed the room, she realized the buffet was all seafood, with meat loaf and vegetable lasagna at opposite ends for those who didn't like seafood.

"Glad you could make it." Marlene appeared at her elbow. "I put you at table one."

"All I see is food." Faith groaned at her own bad joke. "I wouldn't miss a *seafood* buffet for anything." She meant it. The savory odors were making her mouth water.

"I'll keep that in mind." Marlene's tone was dry. "Have fun."

She sped off through the crowd and Faith joined the buffet line. Here she performed the usual juggling act while pouring a cup of clam chowder and filling a plate with fresh shrimp, seafood fettuccine, oysters Rockefeller, and baked haddock plus a heap of salad. Then she staggered along to her table.

Benedict, Sandra, Deb, and another man were seated at table one, eating in silence.

"Hi there." The man waved a greeting and Faith recognized Mark, who had played dead in the garden during a game.

"Hi yourself." Faith set down her dishes and took a seat. "I'm Faith Newberry." She smiled at the others. "Everyone else I know." Benedict stared at his plate, Deb returned her smile, and Sandra nodded, then glanced down at her buzzing phone.

"Nice to officially meet you, Faith." Mark waggled his brows, then pointed at his name tag. "Mark Wilson. Sherlock nerd. My day job is in banking. Boring, right?"

"Money is never boring," Faith said, though secretly she agreed with him.

"Don't listen to him," Deb said. "He's my portfolio diversification manager. And managing my money is never dull."

Sandra gave an exclamation of annoyance. "Sorry, folks. I'd better take this." She grabbed her phone and pushed back from the table.

"Some people never get a break," Mark said. He patted the breast pocket of his jacket. "I turned my phone off."

"You don't need it with your biggest client sitting right beside you," Deb said.

"True, very true." Mark looked thoughtful. "But tonight I only want to think about one thing: winning the scavenger hunt." His eyes gleamed. "Grand prize is first-class tickets to London for an all-expenses-paid Sherlock tour."

"That's a great prize," Faith said. "And this meal is wonderful." She scooped up the last spoonful of creamy chowder.

"We have some generous sponsors," Benedict said.

Deb ducked her head and Faith wondered if she was one of them. Sandra returned with a flurry of skirts and a heavy sigh. "I can't wait to retire," she said. "Working for a city is one hassle after another."

"Philistines, all," Benedict said. "They don't value the importance of libraries as a bulwark against the decline of civilization."

His tactful comment earned a smile from Sandra. "You're exactly right," she said, attacking her dinner with gusto. "Maybe I'll quote you."

The dinner entertainment featured a ventriloquist with a Sherlock Holmes doll, a corny comedian, and a duo singing Victorian dance hall tunes. After the last got the entire room singing endless choruses of "Daisy Bell (Bicycle Built for Two)," Faith was eager for the scavenger hunt to start. Anything to escape Sherlock mania at full strength.

Finally Marlene took the stage. "All right, everyone. Let's give the entertainers another round of applause."

The audience dutifully responded with clapping, hoots, and cheers as the performers took a final bow.

"I hope you've eaten enough," Marlene said to groans, "because you'll need all of your energy for our next activity." She went on to explain that each team would get a different set of clues to follow. Also each would randomly lose members at every challenge station, leaving only one or two at the end. If a team couldn't solve a clue, they were all eliminated on the spot.

"Wow, this sounds tough." Mark gazed around the table. "I hope you're all up to it."

Sandra, still looking at her phone, didn't even respond. Benedict was staring morosely into space, and only Deb seemed interested at all. As for Faith, she hoped to get booted right away so she could go home and read with Watson snuggled by her side.

"Anyone who is eliminated should come back here," Marlene said. "There'll be some consolation prizes, many of them quite good." People cheered.

Assistants passed out cloth sacks for booty, flashlights, and whistles, the last two giving Faith pause. Apparently they would be going outside and into dark places. Then envelopes were delivered to each table. Mark snatched it up and ripped it open. "'This dame could give Sir Arthur a run for his money,'" he read. "'She certainly made more.'" He scratched his chin. "What the heck?"

"That's easy," Sandra said. "Dame Agatha Christie."

"Oh yeah." Mark leaped up. "Are you all coming?"

The group trouped out of the banquet hall, through the lobby, and into the Main Hall, where the statue stood. Other teams flitted and ran around the building or ran outside with shouts and laughter. In contrast, her group reminded Faith of depressed ducklings, the four of them trailing quietly behind Mark.

Dame Agatha held envelopes in her carved hand, and a bundle of toy money and a key sat at her feet. After putting the money in the booty sack, Mark climbed up to retrieve the envelopes. He opened the one labeled "Open me first," pulled out a piece of paper, and read it out loud. "'Look for a velvet bag.'"

"Could this be it?" Benedict held up a small black cloth drawstring bag.

"It must be." Mark reached for it, somehow having become the de facto leader of their little band. Inside were eight fake coins, seven gold and one silver. "I get it. Whoever gets the silver coin is out." Mark pulled out three of the gold coins, then shook the sack. He held it out to Sandra first. "Pick one."

Sandra's was gold and Mark next extended the sack to Deb. Benedict ended up with the silver. He held it up for view. "I'm out of the game, folks. Good night and good luck." With that, he strode away across the hall, surprisingly jaunty for someone who had been so gloomy earlier.

Faith turned back to Mark. "What does the clue say?" She hoped she would be next to leave the game.

He opened the second envelope. "'The Cask of Amontillado has nothing on this barrel.'"

"Is that fair, using an Edgar Allen Poe reference?" Sandra asked.

"I guess they had to get creative," Deb said. "Anyway, that sounds like a trip to the wine cellar."

"Where's that?" Faith asked. The house plans confiscated by the police would have been handy right now.

"I have no idea," Deb said, "but we'll find out." She gestured. "Follow me." Deb stopped the first food service employee they passed and soon they were on the lower level, walking past the kitchen and the laundries down a gloomy corridor. The distance between wall sconces required them to use their flashlights.

Faith shone her beam along the wall. As she suspected, someone had unscrewed some of the bulbs, since there they sat, dark in their sockets.

"Could this be any farther?" Mark asked. "I feel like I'm inside a dungeon."

"That's probably the idea," Sandra said. "They wanted to make it fun."

This wasn't Faith's idea of fun but she bit her tongue. Finally, reaching a dead end, they encountered a thick wooden door with a keyhole.

Mark brandished the key found inside the clue envelope. "Want to bet it works?" When he inserted the key, it turned with a satisfactory *click*.

The wine cellar, although clean and free from cobwebs, was obviously a relic of the past. Wine racks were empty except for one or two antique bottles. At one end, in the deepest, darkest corner, sat a huge, ancient cask with a hole where the tap used to be. An empty wine bottle sealed with a cork sat in front of it.

"Someone liked to buy in bulk," Faith said. The others broke into laughter, which broke the tension.

"Don't tell me the clue is inside that thing." Sandra regarded it dubiously. "I'm not sticking my hand inside there for anything."

"Not even tickets to London?" Mark hunkered in front of the barrel and shone his light into the opening. "No spiders or mice I can see. Just an envelope and another one of those sacks. Here goes." He thrust his hand inside and grabbed them.

This sack held eight wine corks of the same size, one marked with a red *X*. Mark adjusted the number again and this time Deb drew the short straw. She saluted. "I'm out of here. See you all later."

After her footsteps died away, Mark opened the clue. "'Perchance to sit and dream where the fairies dance.'" He frowned. "What the heck does that mean?"

Sandra grabbed his arm. "I know. There's a fountain with a statue of Titania in the garden."

"From *A Midsummer Night's Dream*," Faith said. The clues were pretty clever.

Mark picked up the corked bottle. "There's a piece of paper in it. It must be our prize." He thrust it into the booty sack.

Sandra bustled toward the doorway. "Let's go. I need some fresh air." As she reached the doorway, her cell phone gave a shrill ring, making them all jump.

"You have service down here? I've got to change providers," Mark said.

They all laughed, then Sandra put her phone on ignore. "I'll still be out of a job tomorrow, so who cares," she muttered. She glanced up at Mark and Faith, who were both staring at her in shock. "Don't worry about it. I have other options." She tossed her head and led the way out of the cellar.

As they retraced their steps up the corridor and past the working area of the mansion, Faith pondered Sandra's situation. It sounded like the trouble at the library hadn't died down after all. Despite her brave words, Faith knew good positions in the library world weren't easy to come by. Had Sandra lashed out at Doris, blaming her?

In the garden, the Titania fountain still trickled water, though Faith supposed they'd soon have to shut it off for the winter. The pretty piece was in a grassy enclave surrounded by a hedge. In her flashlight's beam, Faith saw dormant flower beds mulched for the season and a couple of wrought iron benches. The statue wore something extra, a sparkly tiara. The prize.

This time Sandra was eliminated with a red button, and Faith and Mark were the last two standing. The clue read, "What a tangled maze we weave in search of success."

"Isn't it 'tangled web'?" Mark asked.

"Yes, usually," Faith said. "I think this means we need to go into the maze." Trepidation panged. Finding the way through a maze was hard enough in daylight, but at night? "I don't know if we should do this."

"Why not?" Mark gestured. "Come on. What's the worst thing that can happen? We get lost?"

Fifteen minutes later, judging by the muttering coming from Mark's direction, Faith knew he now shared her concern. The tall clipped hedges stretched endlessly—until they turned, leading them into yet another dead end. Inside the maze it was dead quiet, the sound of the ocean muffled by the thick evergreens.

"Why didn't I bring bread crumbs? Or string?" Mark said.

Faith had an idea. "Why don't we use some of that fake money? We'll place a bill near the dead end avenues so we don't go down them again."

"Good idea." Mark dug the bundle out of the sack. "We can use pebbles or branches to hold the paper down."

They explored a little longer, marking their route. The turns grew tighter as they approached the center of the maze. Mark rounded a corner, calling out, "We made it."

Faith heard a grunt and Mark's flashlight flew in an arc of light, landing on the other side of the hedge. She rushed forward, heedless of the poor footing. "Mark? Are you all right?"

Something like a bag or cloak came down over her head and shoulders, muffling and blinding her. Faith flailed, trying to get the heavy cloth off. It felt huge and endless and was so thick that sweat sprang out on her neck. She was suffocating.

Strong arms gripped her around the shoulders, forcing her to stop moving. A voice next to her ear whispered harshly. "Quit snooping or this will be your final chapter."

16

Hands pushed Faith hard, sending her into the springy branches of the hedge. She floundered forward, then bounced back and landed with a thud on the ground. Ignoring the throbbing in her shoulder and side, she scratched frantically at the material until she felt fresh air strike her body. She gulped in deep breaths, trembling with shock.

"Faith. Faith. Where are you?" A man's voice called out, a flashlight's beam dancing over the hedges. Wolfe.

"Here, I'm right here." Faith crossed her arms and rested her head on her knees.

Running footsteps approached and a moment later, Wolfe hunkered down beside her. "What happened? Are you all right?"

Faith glanced up at his handsome face, half in light, half in shadow. "Someone covered me with a blanket and then pushed me down." An instinct made her omit the threat. She tugged at the coarse wool still half-covering her, dragging it into the light. "See? Other than that, I'm okay. A little shaken up and definitely bruised, but I'll live."

His head reared back in disbelief. "Someone pushed you down? Who would do such a thing?"

"That's what I'm asking myself," Faith said tartly. She remembered Mark. Had he also been attacked? "Mark Wilson is around the corner. I think he might be hurt."

"Stay right here." Wolfe jumped to his feet and ran down the path. A moment later, he gave a shout of alarm before he started talking into his cell phone. "Is this 911? Wolfe Jaxon here. I've got a guest with a head injury—"

Poor Mark. Using the arm and leg that hadn't hit the ground, Faith levered herself upright with a few groans and grunts. Deciding that the blanket provided necessary warmth against the chilly evening, she draped it around her shoulders and limped to join Wolfe.

He was kneeling beside Mark, pressing a handkerchief to the banker's head while using his shoulder to hold the phone to his ear. With a shrug and a quick movement of one hand, he placed the phone on the grass. "They'll be right here. Call the front desk, won't you, so Marlene can lead them in?"

Faith reached for his phone. "Marlene knows the way to the middle?" By the light of Wolfe's flashlight, she saw they were in a small circular area, a tiny gazebo marking the exact center of the maze.

"Yes, along with most of the staff." He shot Faith a glance. "It's not that hard to figure out in daylight."

After Faith made the call, she lowered herself to the ground on Mark's other side. "Is he going to be all right?"

"I hope so." Wolfe lifted the handkerchief a bit. "The bleeding has slowed but I'm not happy that he's unconscious."

As if in response, Mark groaned and opened his eyes.

Faith almost swooned with relief. "Thank God."

Mark started to lift his head, then winced and groaned. "Oh . . ."

"Don't move, Mark." Wolfe said. "You've been hurt."

"What happened?" Faith asked.

"I tripped over something and fell. That's all I remember."

Tripped or was pushed? Faith glanced around the clearing but she didn't see anything obvious that might have tripped him. She did see a rock or two protruding from the grass. Maybe he'd hit his head on one of them.

Shouts echoed and light beamed through the hedges. "Here come the EMTs," Wolfe said. He patted Mark's shoulder. "You'll be out of here in no time."

A little later, Faith and Wolfe followed the medical personnel and Marlene out of the maze. Although Mark was much better, Wolfe insisted he go to the hospital to be examined. An EMT had checked Faith over at Wolfe's insistence and the verdict was as Faith thought—nothing broken, but she'd have bruises for certain.

"Wolfe," Faith asked as she hobbled her way along the hedge corridors, "why did you come looking for me?" The timing seemed odd and she couldn't shake her disquiet around his sudden appearance.

"Deb Cabot called me," he said. "She said you and Mark had gone into the maze quite a while ago and she was worried you were lost."

She was right. "I'm glad she did. Otherwise we'd both be crawling out. We might have made it by morning. Maybe."

He threw her a sharp look but didn't comment on her sarcasm. "I wonder who wrote the clues. It wasn't a good idea to send you into the maze at night.

"We had flashlights." She halted. "Oh no. Mine must be on the ground somewhere."

"Don't worry about it. I'll send a gardener to look for it tomorrow."

Maybe I'll come back myself and see what I can find. If I can walk, that is.

At Wolfe's insistence, Faith took the next day off. Thanks to a hot bath and twelve hours of sleep, she only ached a little when she finally rolled out of bed.

"Take a look at these black-and-blues, Watson." Faith pulled up her pajama top to display the bruise running down her side. "I hit the ground pretty hard." Thank goodness she hadn't hit her head, like Mark, who fortunately was expected to recover fully.

Blinking balefully, Watson surveyed her bruises and then leaped down from the bed with a meow and rubbed against her legs. Faith crouched with a groan and patted him. "I love you too, Watson. Now let's have breakfast."

Later, dressed in jeans, sneakers, and a fleece jacket, Faith stepped outside. It was another sparkling-clear day, with only a few clouds floating in the deep blue sky. But the breeze was cool and she pulled her collar up around her neck.

Time to go into the maze. Faith was glad to see that no one else was in the garden right now, although off in the distance, a riding lawn mower roared. If she did run into anyone near the site, she planned to say she was looking for her flashlight.

As she wound her way through topiaries, skirted the Titania fountain, and stepped along gravel paths in the formal garden, she thought about the events of the previous night. The police accompanied the ambulance called for Mark, and Faith had found herself relating the incident to Officer Rooney.

For a change, the officer had been sympathetic and had even insisted on taking photographs of Faith's bruises. "Be careful, Miss Newberry," she had said as she finished her write-up. "Don't go wandering around at night, okay?" Then she had narrowed her eyes. "Can you think of any reason why someone would do such a thing?"

Faith had squirmed, not wanting to relay the threat. If the police learned she'd been poking around into the murder investigation, they wouldn't be happy. She didn't even dare to inquire about its status, not as long as she was still a suspect.

"I have no idea," she had finally muttered.

Rooney's stern expression had perfectly conveyed doubt and suspicion. "If you think of anything, let me know." She had slapped her book shut. "In the meantime, stay away from isolated places."

The officer's advice came to mind as Faith approached the maze, but in daylight, it appeared harmless, only an inviting network of hedges, not a place of threat. Faith found her way easily, helped by the dew-soaked play money they'd left the night before at critical points.

She thought about gathering the bills as she went but decided to wait until the way out. *Better to be cautious, right?*

In the center of the maze, Faith stopped and studied the gazebo. It was barely big enough for two people, like a wedding cake topper of a pavilion. A paper bag sat on the floor—the final clue, she guessed.

Inside was a vintage Rubik's Cube, a once-popular puzzle requiring the player to line up sections by color, and a note. "Congratulations, you've survived the quest," it read. "Take this and the rest of your prizes to contest headquarters."

Faith set the bag down, deciding to collect it later. Maybe the contest organizers would still allow Mark to enter the big prize drawing. Taking a deep breath, she retraced her steps to where she'd been assaulted.

Had the attacker followed them? Or had he been waiting? Forcing the scary memory out of her mind, she focused on scouring the ground and bushes nearby. She found her flashlight and tucked it into her pocket.

In a little cul-de-sac near the path, she spotted something white under the hedge. Kneeling to look, she found two cigarette butts. She pictured the assailant standing in the dark, smoking to keep himself occupied.

Faith found a wrinkled but clean tissue in her jacket pocket and used that to pick up the butts. She wrapped them up and tucked them into a zippered pocket, realizing as she did so that they may have lain there for days, tossed aside by another visitor.

After leaving the maze, she spotted one of the gardeners raking a gravel path. Young and fit, he wore jeans and a Castleton Manor polo shirt embroidered with his name, Eban. "It must be a lot of work keeping up these gardens," she said after greeting him. "But they're gorgeous."

"Aren't they?" Eban's smile was wide and friendly. "I'm doing a paper on the designer for my landscape architecture class." He gestured at nearby topiaries. "The gardens haven't really changed since the late 1800s, when they were built."

"Can't improve on perfection," Faith said. "I have a question.

Where can I throw something away?" She patted her pocket. "I picked up some trash in the maze."

"Sorry about that. We check the grounds every day for litter." Eban nodded at a bin attached to the nearby mower. "You can toss it in there."

There was her answer. The cigarette butts had most likely been left the night before. "Thanks." She turned to go, then thought of something. "Is there a path down to the water from the cliffs?"

"There is." He pointed to a nearby intersection. "The perimeter path skirts the edge. A little way along you'll see a set of stairs leading down to the beach." He shrugged. "It's not much of a beach but you can walk on it at low tide."

"Thanks again." With a wave, she headed toward the path, pausing at the bin to pretend to throw away something. Inside was a collection of cans and bottles along with paper and wrappers. Keeping the grounds clean must take constant vigilance.

Faith strolled along the perimeter path, enjoying the view of the water. She couldn't believe she hadn't gone down to the beach yet. Normally that would have been one of her first stops. *But everything is far from normal here.*

Halfway along the mansion's property, she found the stairs as Eban promised. They led steeply down the cliffs in several sections, and to her relief, appeared sturdy and safe. As he said, the beach was only a strip of rocky sand, bordered on both ends with rocky outcroppings. But it was waterfront within walking distance of her home, a real treat.

She started down the stairs, her heart beating a little faster in anticipation. One of her passions was spending time on the shore, allowing the wash of waves and the vista of endless sky and water to soothe her soul. Sometimes she hunted for shells or searched tide pools for minnows or crabs.

Halfway down, she spotted a couple coming around one of the outcroppings. The man was tall and lanky; the woman, a short blonde.

She squinted her eyes against the bright sunlight, trying to get a better look, then pulled out her sunglasses. As they drew closer, she recognized Marlene Russell. Her companion was a stranger.

The couple didn't appear to notice her as she continued down the stairs. Stopping partway along the beach, they began to argue, their words muffled by the wind and roar of the surf. But Faith recognized the body language of a fight. Marlene leaned forward, both fists clenched at her side, and the man scowled and hunched his shoulders.

She hesitated, wondering if she should retreat and pretend she hadn't seen them. Before she could decide, the pair separated, Marlene marching across the beach toward the stairs. The man slouched along the water, heading toward the other outcropping.

Realizing it was too late, Faith continued to the bottom of the steps. Marlene kept her head down, watching her feet as she trudged through the soft sand. "Hi, Marlene," Faith said when she came within earshot.

Marlene jerked up her head with a glare and Faith saw the sparkle of tears in her eyes. "What are *you* doing here?"

Faith shrugged. "Enjoying the beach. I can't believe I haven't been down here before now. It's beautiful."

Marlene grunted. "It's okay. You can't swim here. The current is too strong."

"Thanks for the warning." Faith moved closer. "Marlene, is everything all right?"

The manager pulled a tissue out of her pocket and wiped her eyes angrily. "Why wouldn't it be?" She pushed past Faith toward the stairs. "Come see me this afternoon at four. We need to talk about how we can improve things for the next retreat."

17

So much for a day off. Faith didn't argue, however, realizing that Marlene was embarrassed by her show of emotion and was covering it up with anger. Plus the mention of the next retreat meant she wasn't about to be fired—yet. Partway down the beach, Faith found a warm spot hidden in the shelter of a big rock and sat down, absorbing the sunshine and watching the waves roll in. Seagulls squawked, landing nearby to stalk around and regard her with beady eyes, heads jerking. Next time she'd bring some bread to feed them.

In the distance, a small dog came trotting along the sand, stopping here and there to sniff. Molly. Benedict followed, pausing to pull out a pack of cigarettes and light one, his ever-present cloak swinging from his shoulders.

Benedict Sinclaire was a smoker? Faith shrank back against the rock face, hoping he wouldn't see her. *Had he hidden in the maze last night?* He could have, since he was dismissed from the team in the first round. He was also tall and strong, with long arms, like her attacker. *Like Wolfe. But Wolfe didn't smoke. Or did he?* What did she really know about any of these people except what they chose to display?

"Molly, come." Benedict whistled, summoning the dog from her investigation of seaweed washed up on the beach. Still smoking, he sauntered along the beach, his route leading the duo right past where Faith was sitting.

She scooted back into the shadows under an overhang. She should be invisible here unless he looked directly into the alcove. A few moments later, he went past, his gaze fixed on the water.

The dog. Molly snuffled along the sand behind him like a miniature bloodhound, obviously scenting something very interesting. She lifted her head and stared at Faith. "Woof." Tongue hanging out, she bolted toward Faith in joy, glad to see a friend.

Faith made a shooing motion with her hands. "Go on, go."

No such luck. The dog, hindquarters twitching as she wagged her tail, jumped on Faith's lap and licked her face.

"Molly. Molly. Where are you, girl?"

Molly turned toward her master's voice but she didn't budge. Benedict returned, scanning the beach for his pet. When he got close, she jumped off Faith's lap and ran toward him, leaping up onto his legs.

He fondled her head. "There you are. I was wondering where you went." Glancing up, he spotted Faith, recoiling slightly. "Faith. I didn't see you sitting there." To her unease, he walked toward her, the dog at his heels. A day ago she would have welcomed his company. Now she didn't trust him—or anyone.

"This is the first time I've been down here," she said, praying he wouldn't linger. "It's nice."

"Doris and I used to take walks on the beach." Benedict took a final drag and put out his cigarette, crushing it with his shoe. For a moment Faith hoped she could retrieve it to compare with the others, but he bent down and picked up the butt, checking to make sure it was out. He stepped closer. "I heard you had a little trouble last night."

"I guess you could say that. Mark fell and hit his head."

Benedict's expression was rueful. "That's too bad. He probably let his enthusiasm get the best of him, running around in the dark like that. He was acting like a big kid."

"Nothing wrong with that. He was having fun."

Benedict fished for his cigarettes and pulled out another, then lit it.

"I didn't know you were a smoker," Faith said.

He took a deep drag. "I'm not. This is a temporary lapse. Brought on by stress." He frowned. "I heard someone attacked you. Are you okay?" Was he really concerned or fishing for information?

Faith shifted, bringing her legs up in front of her. "I'm fine. Someone scared me, that's all." She picked up a stick and began to draw in the sand. "It was just a prank."

"Really?" Cocking his head, he squinted at her. "What happened?"

Shouts and screams came from the beach and Benedict and Faith turned to look. A group from the retreat were clustered at the shore, laughing at one of the men, who had rolled up his pant legs and waded into the icy water.

Faith used the distraction as an opportunity to escape. Dropping the stick, she quickly stood and brushed off the seat of her jeans. "I've got a meeting so I'd better get back. See you later." She felt his eyes on her back as she hurried toward the stairs, moving as fast as she could in the shifting sand.

The tightening of her nerves told her the situation was rising to a head. How much longer could she navigate these dangerous waters?

"Knock, knock, special delivery," Faith called, accentuating her words with a rap on Mark's room door. After leaving early for her meeting with Marlene, Faith had taken a detour into the maze to grab the bag holding the Rubik's Cube.

The door opened and to Faith's surprise, librarian Sandra Baker stood there. "Come on in and join the party." Sandra smiled but Faith noticed lines of strain around her eyes.

"How are you doing?" Deb Cabot turned around in her chair to ask.

"I'm fine," Faith said. "I wanted to see how you were, Mark."

Mark gestured at the bandage on his head. "Still have a bit of a headache but I'll live." He sat on a sofa near a window with an ocean view and Sandra plopped down beside him, leaving the second armchair for Faith. Although not as plush as the suites, the retreat's standard rooms were gorgeous, Faith noticed.

Faith handed Mark the bag she was carrying. "I found this in the maze."

His eyes lit up as he reached inside and pulled out the cube. "The last clue *was* there." He frowned. "Too bad we missed the deadline."

Faith grinned. "No we didn't. I prevailed on the contest organizers for an extension. We're still in it for the grand prize."

"Oh yes, they're giving those out tomorrow night at the banquet," Deb said. "So that worked out perfectly."

Mark set the bag on the coffee table, next to a tray holding a carafe and several cups. "Thanks, Faith. You're a great partner." Sandra cleared her throat and rolled her eyes, attracting his attention. He laughed. "You're all great, really."

"Good thing you said that," Deb said in mock anger. She glanced at her watch. "I've got to go. Clancy needs his walk."

"I'll go with you," Sandra said, rising to her feet. "I can use the exercise."

After the door shut behind them, Mark asked, "Do you have time for a cup of coffee?"

Faith looked at her own watch. "Actually I do. Thanks." She'd have to keep an eye on the time. Marlene didn't like people being late for meetings.

Mark poured her a cup and refilled his own. They both doctored their coffee, sitting in silence while Faith racked her brain about how to raise her questions concerning the incident in the maze.

He glanced at the door as though to make sure they really were alone. "I didn't just happen to trip and fall."

Faith studied the banker's face, usually amiable but now set in grim lines. "What do you mean?"

Mark's hand flew to his bandage, touching it lightly with a wince. "I'm not really sure. I was moving pretty fast, then suddenly something was right in front of me. It caught me in the shins and I fell flat on my face. Me hitting my head was a bonus for whoever did it."

"I didn't see anything that could have tripped you when I checked out the maze today," Faith said. "I think you're right." Her assailant must have attacked Mark to get him out of the way.

"Deb and Sandra said something happened to you too?" Mark looked concerned.

Faith took him through the sequence of events, from hearing him cry out to being pushed into the bushes and falling to the ground. Again, caution made her omit the threat. The fewer people who knew she was poking around and were warned about it, the better.

After Faith's revelations, they sipped coffee quietly, both lost in their thoughts. Faith practically ached with the effort of watching everything she said and did. She still wasn't certain who she could trust. Not even Mark, who might have been involved despite his injury.

"You don't think it was one of the rival teams, do you?"

"Are you serious?" Faith bit back a startled laugh.

Mark shook his head sagely. "You never know. That grand prize is a doozy." He winked.

This time Faith didn't hold back her laughter.

Marlene was on the phone when Faith arrived at her office. She could hear her strident tones clearly. "As I said earlier, that's not acceptable to me."

Faith tapped on the door, wanting to warn Marlene that she was there.

"Hold on. My four o'clock is here." Marlene raised her voice. "Come in."

Marlene was still on the phone when Faith slipped in. She glanced up and gestured for Faith to take a seat, then dropped her gaze, frowning. "I really can't talk about it right now. I've got to go, okay?" She clanked the receiver into its cradle.

A knock, then Laura put her head around the partly open door. "Marlene? I'm locked out."

"Again?" With a muffled exclamation, Marlene pushed her rolling chair back. "I'll be right back, Faith." She snatched up her ring of keys and strode out of the room. "That's the third time this week." Marlene's words drifted from the hall. "This is getting old. Really old."

Poor Laura. Today was probably not the time to bring up hiring her as an assistant in the library. Faith sat back in her chair and studied the office. There didn't appear to be a single personal touch anywhere, not a photograph, vase of flowers, memento from a vacation, or a postcard. Unlike Wolfe's office, which had evidence of his sailing passion everywhere. *And a picture of his deceased fiancée right in view.* This glimpse into the millionaire's heart touched Faith. *Could such a man be responsible for murder?* In response all her doubts and conflicting feelings about Wolfe jumbled in her mind until, with a sigh, she turned her attention back to Marlene. The poor woman appeared buried in work. The file cabinets were stacked with files and boxes and the bookshelves behind her desk were also crammed full.

She'd have to take that back about no personal touches. Right there on the desk in front of her, under a heap of binders, was a heart-shaped seashell box. Faith pulled it out, trying not to send the paperwork crashing to the floor.

It was a pretty little thing, better made than most of those sold in tourist traps. The lid, crusted with tiny shells, was hinged, and the interior was lined with red velvet. A slip of paper lay curled inside. With a sinking, heart-thumping awareness that she was prying, Faith picked up the paper and read, *Love you always, babe. Jasper.*

Was Jasper the man she had seen on the beach with Marlene?

Until now, Faith had assumed the manager was a relentlessly single professional woman, without an ounce of girlish romance in her dressed-for-success body.

Marlene's voice sounded from the corridor and Faith hastily closed the box and thrust it back into place. As she did so, the tower of binders slid off the desk in several directions, landing on the floor with a crash.

The door swung open. "What the—" Marlene stared down at Faith, on her knees gathering up the binders.

"I'm sorry. I nudged the pile by accident and they fell over." Scrambling for a reason as to why she was anywhere near the desk, Faith glanced down at the labels. "I wanted to look at this one." She waved it. "The retreat bookings for the year."

Marlene accepted that with a nod, stepping around the books to get to her seat. "I wanted to go over those with you so you know what's coming up."

Order now restored, Faith sat down again. "That's great. I want to have time to read up on the genre or author before each retreat."

The manager settled behind the desk and turned to her computer. "I'll print you a calendar. You don't need the whole binder; that's got my notes on meals, events, and lodging." She pressed a few buttons and the printer began to grind.

"Which are totally fabulous here," Faith said. "I'm going to gain weight if I keep attending functions, not that I don't want to, of course. I mean, I'm happy to go to anything and everything . . ." *Stop it.* She was babbling. What was it about Marlene that made her uncomfortable—besides her gimlet-eyed stare and chilly demeanor, that is?

Marlene turned both on her as she handed Faith several pieces of paper. "Here's the schedule for the year. You can see we're pretty booked up."

Faith glanced down the roster, an idea coming to mind on how to broach the topic of Doris. "You *are* booked. In fact it's rare when you—we—get a week free."

"True. We do pencil in a week or two in the spring to close down and prep for the season. And everyone is off at Christmas and a couple of other holidays. Mrs. Jaxon insisted."

"Very generous." Faith took a breath. "Labor Day weekend is one of them, right?"

"That's right." Marlene busied herself with items on the desk. "We all got a few days off to go play."

"What did you do?" Faith asked casually. "I visited my aunt here in town. We went to a craft fair and ate a lot of lobster."

"Lobster?" Marlene shuddered. "By September I can't even stand the sight of those boiled red things. I rented a room at the beach. Three days of fun in the sun."

Faith froze momentarily. She had caught Marlene red-handed in a lie.

18

Marlene's lie jarred Faith but she regained her composure. "Oh, I love the beach too. Though I have to be careful not to get burned. I've got such fair skin."

"I don't have that problem. I tan. See?" She held out one toasty-brown arm for Faith to admire. She picked up the binder. "Let's go through the retreat calendar month by month."

After browsing through the upcoming events, all of which sounded wonderful, Faith broached another topic. "I've been looking through the special collection, trying to get a handle on what's there."

The other woman raised a brow. "Is there a problem?"

Interesting she asked that. "Not that I've found." Now Faith was lying. "But I'd love to have an expert check everything over. Make sure the books are staying in good condition."

Marlene's glare could have frosted glass. "Isn't that your job?"

"Of course. But we always availed ourselves of second opinions at the college."

The manager gave a huge sigh. "Well, if you must consult someone, give Franklin Woodbury a call. He's our local expert. We use him all the time." She put up a hand, forestalling any comment on her contradictory statements. "When necessary, which isn't often."

"I'll keep him in mind." Faith thought about sharing why she didn't want to work with Franklin but tabled it for the time being. She could always raise the issue with Wolfe and see how he reacted.

"Tomorrow night is the grand finale for this event," Marlene said. "I would like you to participate."

"There's a dinner, right?"

"And a ball. It'd be great if you could come in costume. Everyone else is dressing in period attire."

"You mean a Victorian dress?" Faith laughed. "I hope the corset is optional."

Marlene's brow furrowed. "Your underwear is your business. Just wear a costume, please." She bent to rummage under the desk. "Oh, and take this back to the library, will you? The police dropped it off."

Mortified, Faith stared in dismay at the bound plans for Castleton Manor. She stuttered out a thank-you, grabbed the book, and fled.

Halfway back to the library, her cheeks still warm with embarrassment, Faith had an idea. Why not study the plans in the library? She'd lock the door so no one would interrupt her.

She managed to make it through the main rooms to the library without being stopped by anyone. Inside the warm, quiet enclave, she set the plan book on one of the long tables and sat down with a sigh.

How I love libraries. The towering shelves of books, the smell of leather and paper, the sense that an entire world awaited her inside the volumes . . . this had always been her passion. *And it still is.*

Faith leafed through the plan, careful not to rumple or tear the blueprints. Elevations displayed the architect's vision of the house from every side. Floor plans detailed the room layout, three floors and the basement.

Most houses would be complete with those. But for Castleton Manor, there was another page, one that detailed a network of hidden staircases and tunnels. The alcove where they found Doris had two other doorways in addition to the library—leading upstairs and into the basement. Beyond the wine cellar was a series of small rooms that reminded Faith of a castle's dungeon.

In a time of prosperity and safety, there was no logical reason for someone to build these hiding places and secret passages. Wolfe's great-great-grandfather must have included them for his enjoyment.

The door rattled and Faith glanced up, ready to call out that the library was closed. A key turned in the lock and Wolfe Jaxon entered.

"Oh," they said in unison, then laughed.

What is he doing in here? Faith immediately glanced at the special collection and then chided herself. *He has a right to come in anytime he wants.*

"I thought I told you to stay home today," Wolfe said, striding across the carpet.

Faith thought about throwing her body on top of the plans to hide them, but she realized that would look pretty foolish. "I did. But Marlene wanted to meet with me."

He rolled his eyes. "She's zealous, I have to give her that much. She lives and breathes Castleton Manor."

Faith felt an unexpected pang of sympathy for the manager. "Dedication is a good thing, surely."

"True." Looming over her, he peered down at the book. "What's that you've got there?"

"Plans for the mansion. I thought I'd familiarize myself with the layout."

"Aren't those the ones the police confiscated?"

Warmth flashed over Faith, making her skin prickle with perspiration. "Yes. I took the book home, which I know I shouldn't have—"

He waved a dismissive hand. "I trust you implicitly with our collection. Borrow whatever you want."

"Thanks, Wolfe." To change the subject, she asked, "Do you have any idea where I can find a costume for the dinner and ball? Marlene wants me to attend."

He shook his head. "There's nothing local. You'd have to go to Boston. But I'm sure you can put together something simple without too much trouble."

I'm not so sure of that. Faith closed the plan book and pushed back from the table. "I'd better get started then."

"I think we can cobble together a costume for you," Eileen said. "Can't we, ladies?" She turned to the other members of the Candle House Book Club.

"I have a hat that belonged to my grannie," Midge said. "It has feathers and flowers all over the brim." She gestured to demonstrate.

Brooke tapped her lips, thinking. "How about wearing a short jacket with a long skirt? A lacy blouse under and boots." Her thumbs worked her phone. "See? Like Mary Poppins." She passed around a drawing of the iconic literary figure.

"I have a jacket, boots, and blouse," Faith said.

"And I have a long black skirt." Eileen smiled. "It's my winter dress-up outfit."

"Thanks, everyone." Faith sat back, relieved. "I thought I had to find a ball gown by tomorrow night."

"You don't need a ball gown to look like a character in a Sherlock Holmes story," Eileen said. "So you'll be fine."

Brooke wiggled her fingers at Watson, who had accompanied Faith to the meeting. The cat padded over and wound his way around her legs, purring. "What a sweetie. How's he adjusting to life at Castleton?" Brooke reached down and stroked his chin. Atticus, not to be left out, jumped down from Midge's lap and trotted over for a pat.

"Watson loves living there." Tears sprang to Faith's eyes. "And so do I." She fumbled in her jeans pocket for a tissue, coming up short.

Eileen handed her a clean one. "It will be all right, dear. Don't worry."

"They still haven't found out who killed Doris Lincoln?" Midge shook her head. "For shame."

"No, they haven't." Faith cleared her throat. "And in addition to being a suspect, someone is harassing me." She glanced at her aunt. "There's much more than the broken window in my car."

"There is?" Eileen frowned. "Why didn't you tell me?"

Tears threatened again. "I kept hoping someone would get arrested and put an end to it. Or that I was imagining things." She told them about the watcher in the library and the garden, then relayed the incident in the maze.

Eileen paled. "Things are escalating, Faith. He threatened you and pushed you down?"

"And tripped Mark. He was hurt pretty badly."

"You've got to tell the police." Midge's tone was indignant. "They need to find and arrest whoever it is."

"I did tell them about the assault, but not the threat. I feel like I can't trust anyone." She shook her head. "Not even Wolfe Jaxon. Maybe especially Wolfe Jaxon."

"What do you mean?" Brooke asked. "I thought he was a real straight arrow. Besides being dreamy."

"I thought he was both of those too," Faith said. "But there's something suspicious going on with the book collection." She put up a hand. "You absolutely have to keep this confidential, Brooke. My job depends on it. And since you work at Castleton . . ."

"I get your point. It would be tempting to nose around and ask questions. But I promise I won't say a word." She crossed her heart with a fingertip.

Faith told them about the fake book and the forged signature. "When I told Marlene Russell I wanted to bring someone in to help me assess the private collection, she suggested Franklin Woodbury. But so far he's been useless."

"Marlene Russell is the assistant manager at the retreat, right?" Midge asked. Her brows puckered. "There's something I heard about that woman . . . I can't quite remember what it is."

"She's pretty dedicated," Faith said. "A workaholic, I'd say. But she did lie about where she was Labor Day weekend. She said she went to the beach for three days and worked on her tan. But it was pouring on Sunday."

"Maybe she just didn't bother to give all the details," Eileen said.

"Could be. That's another terrible side effect of this situation. I feel like everyone is lying." Faith remembered Benedict's tale. "One of the retreat guests, that author Benedict Sinclaire, was Doris's boyfriend. He said they broke up late Saturday night. So I think Doris was killed on Sunday."

"If he's telling the truth," Brooke said. "I've noticed him getting pretty cozy with Sandra Baker." She turned to Eileen and Midge. "She's one of the conference organizers and an attractive librarian."

"He must have a thing for librarians," Midge said. "You'd better be careful, Faith." She wiggled her eyebrows at Faith and everyone laughed.

After the laughter quieted, Faith said, "See what I mean? Everything people do is subject to interpretation, both negative and positive. I did find out that Sandra was angry with Doris. They used to work together and it looks like Sandra might be losing her job because of Doris's complaints."

"Maybe Benedict and Sandra conspired to kill Doris." Brooke's eyes were wide.

"Let me tell you something else about the maze incident," Faith said. "I found some cigarette butts near where I was attacked. And then today I found out that Benedict smokes."

Brooke bounced in her seat. "See? That proves it."

"Let's not speculate," Eileen said. "Faith, I think you need to tell all this to the police. Let them sort it out." She picked up the book they were discussing this week. "I know it probably seems tame by comparison, but let's discuss this mystery."

It was midmorning the next day before Faith worked up the courage to call the police. She couldn't shake the feeling that they would regard anything she said as an attempt to get off the hook.

Faith cringed when Officer Rooney came on the line. "Miss Newberry. What do you have for me?"

Faith took a deep breath and plunged in, deciding to start with something fairly easy. "I found out Doris Lincoln's ex-boyfriend smokes. Benedict Sinclaire."

She heard a sound suspiciously like muffled laughter. "And that's relevant why?"

"I found cigarette butts in the maze. I think my attacker was smoking while he waited for me to come along."

"Did you smell smoke on his person? Or her person. Let's not make assumptions."

"I believe it was a man and no, he didn't smell of cigarette smoke. My head was covered with a blanket, remember? And I also think the incident is connected to Doris Lincoln's death."

"And why is that?"

It took a couple of tries but Faith finally forced the words out. "Because he threatened me. 'Quit snooping or this will be your final chapter.'"

Silence for a few seconds. "How literary of him." Rooney's tone was dry. "Have you been snooping?"

"No, not really. I did find out Marlene Russell lied about going to the beach. And Sandra Baker is losing her job because of Doris Lincoln. And there are a lot of strange things going on here—"

"Save it, Miss Newberry. And stay out of the way of our investigation."

Faith stared at the phone for a minute, stung by Officer Rooney's response. *Oh well, I tried to do my duty* . . . Forcibly pushing all thoughts of Doris Lincoln and the Castleton Manor library out of her mind, Faith ran a bubble bath. She might as well make a special occasion out of the dinner and ball since she was required to attend.

After a long and leisurely bath, Watson supervising from the toilet lid, Faith piled up her hair and applied more makeup than usual. The Victorian outfit was quite fetching, especially when she added the hat, attaching it to her hair with bobby pins.

"I don't happen to have a hatpin, Watson. They probably don't even make them anymore." The cat watched her every move from his perch on the bed. "Bobby pins will have to do." She pushed at the hat experimentally. "That should hold unless I'm in a really strong wind."

At the front door, Watson attempted to push past her legs. Faith blocked him with one foot. "You can't come with me tonight. I'm sorry." He stared up at her, unblinking, but she didn't relent. Edging carefully out the door, she said, "Don't worry. I'll be back soon."

As she pulled the door shut, a black-and-white streak zoomed by. He was gone. "Be careful, Watson," she called.

The cat waited behind a bush as his human strode down the path, humming under her breath. Her long skirt swayed as she walked and for a moment he was tempted to run after her and attack it, just for fun.

But then she'd put him back inside . . . and he refused to be locked up tonight. He left the shelter of the foliage and followed, swinging his head back and forth to scan the shadows.

Bad things lurked in this garden—things that tried to hide, to blend into the pools of darkness at the edges. There was one now, standing near the elephant topiary.

The figure in the cloak watched his human.

And Watson watched him.

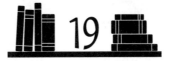

19

The banquet hall had been transformed into something from a Victorian novel. The long tables were set with white linen and silver and lined with candelabras and vases of flowers. Servers dressed in formal vintage garb circulated, offering appetizers to the guests standing in groups around the room.

An especially unusual touch was the employee assigned to announce each guest at the doorway. "Name, please."

"Faith Newberry."

"Miss or Mrs.?" He winked. "Or is it Lady?"

"Plain old Miss."

"Miss Newberry!" he bellowed. A few heads turned, took Faith in, then went back to their chatter. To her amusement, she noticed about half a dozen or more Sherlock capes among the black and tweed suits. The women wore a range of styles, from prim serge suits to ball gowns.

Faith was pleased to see Brooke coming her way, holding a small tray aloft on one hand. "Do you believe this?" Brooke tugged at the long skirt of her maid costume with the other hand. A white cap perched on her head. "We had to dress up too." She surveyed Faith from head to toe. "You look awesome."

"Thanks. So do you." Faith selected a cold shrimp from the pile on Brooke's tray and dipped it in sauce. "What's the menu tonight?"

"Roast beef and Yorkshire pudding, what else? Oh, and trifle for dessert."

Faith's belly rumbled. "That sounds great." Brooke moved away with a smile. A dinner gong sounded, the mellow tone echoing through the room. People began to move toward the tables.

"Good evening, Faith," boomed a deep voice behind her.

She turned to see Wolfe Jaxon, wearing his Sherlock cape and carrying an unlit pipe. "Hello, Wolfe. I see you're dressed in the spirit of the occasion."

"As are you. Good show, as the Brits say." Wolfe glanced over her costume and then leaned close. "If you have time after dinner, I have something to show you regarding our joint family history."

Faith laughed. "How can I refuse such an intriguing invitation? I'd love to see it."

"Come find me after dessert, all right?"

As they approached the tables, Wolfe broke away with a swirl of his cloak and aimed for the head table, where he joined the organizing committee and Mark, still sporting a bandage. Faith, to her amusement, was seated at the far end of the room, near the service door. She was placed "below the salt," as the old-fashioned phrase went.

At each setting was a menu card, proclaiming the meal to be in the "style and spirit of Victorian England." After a welcome and retreat recap from Sandra, the meal began with leek and potato soup, followed by a salad with beets and radishes. Then, with fanfare, a carving station was wheeled out and a giant roast was sliced and served, along with golden squares of Yorkshire pudding and pitchers of gravy.

Faith's tablemates joked and commented, and while she nodded or chuckled in the right places, her thoughts were consumed by Wolfe's words. What was he going to show her? Could it have something to do with the ship's logbooks she had seen in his office? And why now? Eating absently, she managed to tuck away most of her meal. But she did refuse the trifle, a concoction of ladyfingers, custard, jam, and whipped cream, due to the tightness of the borrowed skirt's waistband.

After dessert, Sandra went to the podium again to announce dancing in the Main Hall. Prizes would be awarded throughout the event, and at midnight, snacks would be served. This last was met with general laughter and groans.

"I don't know if I can move, let alone dance," Faith overheard one woman say when the dinner adjourned for dancing in the Main Hall. "I ate too much."

"I'm looking forward to working all these calories off," said another. "Come on, it will be fun."

During the general exodus, Wolfe made his way to Faith's side. "Do you still want to go up and see what I found?"

"I'd love to. Lead on." Although she was eager to solve the family mystery, trepidation panged as she trailed behind Wolfe's broad-shouldered figure, striding with confidence toward the staircase. She thought again of cloaked figures watching and strong arms gripping her in the maze. *Had he really suddenly discovered something? Or did he have something else in mind for her?*

Brooke passed by, raising her brows at the sight of Faith and her escort heading the opposite direction from the rest of the crowd.

Faith darted to her friend's side. "I'm going up to Wolfe's office to see some historical documents regarding my ancestor," she whispered.

"And you wanted someone to know." Brooke nodded. "Got it."

Wolfe stopped, turning to see where Faith was. With a wave, Faith hurried to join him. "Sorry. I wanted to compliment Brooke on the meal. It was fantastic."

He began to trudge up the steps. "We pride ourselves on our food. I think it goes a long way to making people want to come back."

"You mean besides this gorgeous mansion located right on the ocean? And the excellent programs you put on?" Faith heard herself gushing, something she sometimes did when she was nervous.

"This has to be one of the best book retreat venues in the country."

"I'm glad you think so. My mother came up with the idea. It's a good use for a property that otherwise would be too expensive to justify keeping."

Were the Jaxons supplementing their coffers by selling rare books? "There must be tons of upkeep."

"Yes, and we employ a pretty big staff year round. Even before we started the retreat. Some people try to get by with part-timers and that doesn't work." Wolfe unlocked the door to his apartment, standing back to let Faith pass.

After he shut the thick door, Faith felt a sudden sense of isolation. *I'm alone up here with Wolfe. Now what?* No noise from the lively ball downstairs penetrated and it was deathly quiet. Only a lamp here and there lit the spacious room, and beyond the huge windows, the lights of a passing freighter gleamed on the inky horizon. Stars glittered above.

She briefly considered leaving, imagining herself running down to the warm, convivial atmosphere awaiting her in the Main Hall.

Wolfe moved to her side. "Even at night the view is spectacular from up here. I never get tired of it."

"It is amazing." Faith took a step away, disconcerted by his closeness, every molecule of her body urging her to escape. She took a deep breath. "So what was it you wanted to show me?"

"It's in the office. Follow me." Wolfe paused to take off his cape and throw it over the back of a sofa. "This thing is sweltering."

"I can imagine. I'm not used to long skirts either."

He glanced over his shoulder. "But you do look lovely. I especially like the hat."

Flattered despite her uneasiness, Faith touched the brim, adjusting the hat's placement on her head. "Something else I'm not used to wearing."

"Me neither. I drew the line at a deerstalker cap." Wolfe flipped the light switch inside the office. "Our conversation the other day made me curious about what happened on Angus Jaxon's ship." He pulled out the ship's log Faith had found on her earlier visit.

"You never read it before?" Faith wasn't sure she believed him.

"Not before the other day. I usually find old-fashioned and faded handwriting tedious." He set the book on the desk and leafed through with gentle fingers.

"It can be hard to interpret. Especially if the spelling is inconsistent."

"Or when an *s* looks like an *f*." He stopped turning pages. "Ah, here we are. June 1825." He moved the book over so Faith could see the entry.

Wolfe began to read, squinting and hesitating in certain places.

> *We experienced a great tragedy today, the loss of a good friend and companion, Josiah Newberry. If it weren't for the confidential nature of this log, I would hesitate to record this sad story. It is one of those instances where the public tale must differ from the truth, but in this case such subterfuge is of the greatest necessity.*

"My goodness," Faith said. "He was long-winded."

"I know," Wolfe said. "I was, like, get to the point already." He cleared his throat.

> *Josiah suffered one of the greatest betrayals known to man and it broke his spirit. How else can I explain his actions?*

"Angus betrayed him?" Again Faith interrupted.

Wolfe held up a hand. "Not so fast. Someone much dearer to Josiah than Angus.

> *I was on the deck giving instruction to the first mate when we heard a gunshot. Fearing problems among the unruly crew, I hastened below. One of the men told me it had come from my cabin. Heart in my throat, I ventured inside, not knowing what I might find.*

> *Josiah lay dead on the floor, a revolver close to hand. Next to him was a letter. Although I hesitated to breach his privacy even in death, I had to read it.*

Wolfe's voice thickened and he cleared his throat again. "Sorry. For some reason this part chokes me up."

"It is sad. Take your time." That admission thawed Faith's doubts concerning the millionaire. Like the cherished photo of his lost love, his reaction to a two-hundred-year-old tragedy spoke of a soft and caring heart.

> *The letter was from Josiah's wife. She informed him that she loved another man, a situation brought about by his long absences at sea. She hoped that he would forgive her and release her without difficulty or scandal. My dear friend, already in frail mental health due to financial reverses, must have been heartbroken and full of shame. As a result, he took his own life.*

"Angus must have covered up the suicide," Faith said. "The story was that Josiah had been ill and died at sea." She shrugged. "Of course there were also rumors of foul play."

"I can see why. Listen." Wolfe read on.

I called upon my first mate, one of the few men I trust implicitly, and together we bundled Josiah in a sail and stitched it shut. We told the rest of the crew that he died from a pox, something they probably don't believe, but none dared to question us. As I read Holy Scripture for the benefit of Josiah's soul, four men carried him to the railing and sent him to a watery grave. I must now inform his widow—grieving or not—and his children. A terrible business. I am forlorn with grief.

Faith was silent for a long moment after Wolfe's voice died away. The logbook entry cast Angus Jaxon's actions in a benevolent light. Maybe people had sensed there was more to the story and after a generation or two, the details were lost but the suspicion remained. As for Josiah's wife, it was probably easier to lay blame on the Jaxons than carry the guilt of causing her husband's death.

"Thanks for sharing that, Wolfe," Faith said. "It's good to know the real story, even if it is heartbreaking."

Wolfe closed the book and slid it back onto the shelf. "I wanted to put your mind at ease. If we're going to—"

The phone on the desk rang shrilly. With a muffled exclamation of irritation, Wolfe glanced at the display. "Marlene. Sorry. I'd better take this." He snatched up the receiver. "Yes, Marlene."

Faith clearly heard the manager's shrill voice urging Wolfe to attend to an emergency in the kitchen. With a headshake, he hung up. "I'd better go. We'll talk later." Moving decisively, he ushered her out of the office, switching off the light.

As Faith trailed down the stairs to the main floor, Wolfe having hurried on ahead, she wondered about his cutoff sentence. Had he been talking about working together—or something more personal? She scoffed at her foolish thoughts. The last thing she needed was to be involved with her boss.

At the foot of the stairs stood a man wearing a Sherlock cape, picking up what looked like business cards from the floor. "Ah, there you are, Miss Newberry. Don't mind me, I dropped my cards when I tripped over a cat. Animals are everywhere in this place."

Faith recognized Franklin Woodbury, the bookseller. "How are you, Franklin? I didn't see you earlier tonight."

Franklin chuckled as he tucked the cards into his pants pocket. "I just this moment arrived." He gestured to his clothing. "Thought I'd get into the spirit of things."

"Me too." Faith reached the bottom of the flight. "Have you been dancing?" In the Main Hall straight ahead, couples bounced around the dance floor to a lively song.

"I don't dance, I'm afraid. My joints can't take it and besides, I look like a hopping toad."

With a smile at his jest, Faith moved toward the ball, not sure if she wanted to linger. Maybe she could slip out and go home. Marlene was busy with the emergency in the kitchen, so she wouldn't notice Faith's absence.

Franklin fell into step beside her. "I was wondering if we could talk, Miss Newberry. I've learned something interesting about the books you showed me."

Faith stopped dead in surprise. "What is it? Tell me."

The bookseller peered around. "Not here. Let's go to the library where we can have some privacy."

It must be bad news then. Has he learned that Wolfe was involved? Faith's heart sank at the thought. She patted her pockets. "All right. I happen to have the key on me."

They skirted the dance floor to the gallery, where small groups of people and couples were chatting here and there. No one seemed to notice Faith and the bookseller pass by as they made their way to the library.

Faith unlocked the door and stood back to let Franklin precede her into the room. After shutting the door, she turned. "So tell me, what did you find—"

Franklin held a revolver, its shiny barrel pointed right at her heart.

20

Faith gasped, the air leaving her body and making her legs weak. "What . . . what are you doing?" She opened her mouth, mustering the breath to scream.

Franklin waved the gun. "Don't even think about it. No one would hear you anyway. Lock the door and leave the key. I *will* shoot you if I must."

Faith turned the key in the lock, feeling as though she signed her death warrant as she did so. "I don't understand this." *Is he planning to steal the special collection?*

"Shut up." He snatched the key, then waved the gun at the settee in front of the fireplace. "Sit there."

On trembling legs, Faith obeyed. Her thoughts darted around as she sought escape. She could run for the stairs, but he'd shoot her before she made it.

"Take the books. I'm sure they're insured."

"What makes you think that's what I want?" Franklin slapped a piece of duct tape on her mouth and bound her wrists behind her. Keeping one eye on her, he went to the wall and opened the secret doorway. With that movement, Faith knew the truth.

Franklin killed Doris. Screams rose in Faith's chest but they emerged only as muffled grunts and wails.

He darted back to her, moving rapidly for a man with aching joints. "Get up." Faith tried but her knees collapsed and she fell back onto the settee. Tears sprang to her eyes.

He grabbed her arm and pulled her upright, then pushed her toward the opening. "Go on. Get moving."

Faith stumbled forward into the dark space, heels tapping on the stone floor. Cool, stale air closed around her and the memory of finding Doris flashed into her mind. Hysteria threatened, but with an intense, shuddering effort, she managed to slow her breathing and her heart rate. *Don't panic. Just find a way out of this.*

Franklin closed the door, plunging them into utter darkness. Fortunately he switched on a flashlight and, using the beam as a pointer, indicated the route, one of the doorways Faith remembered from the map. It led into the cellars.

Step by step they plodded down a narrow, winding staircase. Franklin kept barking at Faith to hurry, but in the bad light she had to watch every footstep on the narrow, triangular stairs.

At the bottom a corridor extended both ways. Faith pictured the map in her head. To the left was a route to the kitchens and other workrooms; to the right, the dungeon-like rooms. The air underground was damp and musty, and water dripped in a constant echoing *plop . . . plop . . . plop. If the dank isolation didn't drive prisoners mad, that sound would.* But there weren't any prisoners housed at Castleton. *Until now.*

"Turn right." Franklin shone his light in that direction and something skittered into the dark beyond.

Faith moved as slowly as possible, praying someone, anyone would come to rescue her. Overhead the guests danced and partied, unaware that this drama was occurring far below their feet. And what about Wolfe? Would he notice she was missing?

But even if someone had noticed her with Franklin, they'd assume she had gone home. It would be too late . . .

"In there." Franklin indicated a doorway on the left.

Faith entered a small square room resembling a cell. There were no windows except an opening cut into the wooden door. Standing shelves in a corner lined with ancient bottles and cans revealed it had once been used as a storeroom.

"Sit." Franklin pointed to the dusty stone floor.

It was awkward sitting with bound hands, but Faith managed,

thumping down onto the hard surface. She bowed her head and shut her eyes, breathing a prayer. Was it really going to end like this?

The door squeaked shut. Faith opened one eye. She was alone in the dark, and Franklin was gone.

Faith struggled to her knees and stood. Something in the folds of her dress banged her thigh. Her cell phone. Franklin had neglected to search her, an omission she was grateful for.

Using her hands to bunch her skirt to the back, she was able to get the phone out of her pocket. By memory, she found and pressed the side button to turn it on, then twisted around to see if she had service.

Nothing. Apparently the signal couldn't penetrate this far underground.

Voices muttered in the corridor. Someone was coming. Faith hastily turned the phone off and slid it under the shelving.

The door squeaked open. Several figures were outlined by the flashlights two of them were carrying. A shove sent one of the figures staggering into the room.

Marlene Russell. Faith yelped behind the duct tape.

"Don't do this." Marlene's voice was pleading. "I won't tell, I promise."

"Too late," Franklin said. "You're not trustworthy. Right, Jasper?"

Jasper. Where had Faith seen that name? Oh yes, on the love note in the seashell heart. The other person stepped forward, and even in the dim light, Faith recognized the man from the beach, the one who had made Marlene cry.

"Sorry about this, sweetie." Jasper pulled out a roll of tape and bound Marlene's hands. "At least you've got company."

"Company?" Marlene's green gaze skated around the room, landing on Faith, hunkered near the shelves. "Faith Newberry. Why aren't you at the dance?"

Dear Marlene. Even in a crisis it's work first. Faith grunted a reply and with a laugh, Franklin chimed in. "She can't talk right now. Our new librarian was getting a little too close to the truth, I'm afraid."

With a nasty grin, Jasper reached over and pulled the tape off Faith's face. "Now you two can talk shop while you wait."

Faith blinked back tears from the sting of having the tape ripped away from her lips and chin.

"Are you sure that's a good idea?" Franklin asked his accomplice.

"What harm can it do? No one can hear them yell down here." Jasper picked up the tape. "Let's roll."

The door slammed, leaving the women in the dark. Marlene sobbed softly while Faith attempted to reorganize her thoughts. Jasper and Franklin had been working together to steal from the collection, apparently with Marlene's help. "You killed Doris, didn't you?"

The sobbing halted. "I didn't. Those two did."

"But you were there," Faith guessed. "You weren't at the beach."

Marlene gave an audible gulp. "You're right, I wasn't." Her words rushed out as though she was relieved to finally tell someone. "Doris told Franklin she was going to bring in the police to investigate the forgeries."

Faith remembered the librarian's missed appointment with Wolfe. "Why didn't she tell Wolfe?" She edged over to the shelf where her phone lay.

"She was going to, but I convinced her she needed more proof, so she cancelled. Franklin told her he was bringing in an expert to talk to her."

"I'm guessing Jasper played that role."

"You're right." Marlene's laugh was bitter. "Only it wasn't a role. Jasper is the one doing the forgeries. In fact, he just got out of prison. He was in for ten years."

"Is Jasper an old boyfriend of yours?"

"He's my ex-husband," Marlene said. "When I found out he was a forger, I divorced him and tried to start over. But my past followed me."

She noticed the light coming from Faith's cell. "You have a phone?"

"Yes, but there's no signal down here. I'm using it as a flashlight." Faith wiggled her way to her feet, wondering if there was something on the shelves they could use as a weapon. Panting with effort, she asked, "Jasper and Franklin were blackmailing you?"

"Yes. Of course I should have gone to Wolfe right away but I was afraid." She lowered her voice. "You see, I helped Jasper once, when we were married. I didn't do time, but I was on probation for five years."

Not exactly something to include on your résumé. "You were in a tight spot," Faith said, deciding that censure wouldn't help the situation any. The contents of the shelves appeared to be ancient household products.

"After Franklin killed Doris, I knew I had to do something to stop them. Now they're stopping me. And you."

"Tell me what happened with Doris." The cans weren't any good. She needed something that would break.

"We met her at the cottage, like I told you. But she didn't believe Jasper when he said the books were authentic. She threatened to go to the police and when she pulled out her phone, Franklin chased her outside with the fireplace poker." Marlene paused and even in the dark, Faith sensed her fear and anguish. "It was awful. Jasper stopped her and Franklin hit her on the head . . ."

Faith's blood ran cold. "And Franklin and Jasper hid her in the secret room." She and Marlene had to get out of here. She didn't believe for an instant that the partners in forgery—and murder—would let them walk.

On the bottom shelf, in the corner, sat several dusty amber glass jugs. Faith shone the light on them. These weren't labeled, but she could see raised lettering on the glass. Those products would do just fine for what she had in mind. "Marlene, can you free my hands?"

After Marlene tore away the tape binding Faith's hands, she

returned the favor. "Marlene, I noticed you have your keys. By any chance is there one that might work on this door?"

Among the jingling mass on the ring, they found one that fit the ancient door. The cell next to them was empty, so Faith and Marlene hid there with the jugs Faith had found.

They secreted themselves barely in time. The sound of voices and the flickering of flashlights came along the corridor.

"I just can't believe the real *Scarlet* and the signed Conan Doyle aren't in the library somewhere," Franklin said. "Where did your ex put them?"

"I don't know," Jasper said. "But I'm going to find out. This is the second time we've looked through those shelves."

"Let's get it out of her before we . . . you know."

Marlene started. "I think I just figured out where the books are," she whispered.

"Tell me later," Faith whispered back.

The two men passed by the slightly open door of their cell and unlocked the other door. Shouts erupted when they realized the women were gone. Moving quickly, Faith threw open the door and lobbed jugs through the open doorway of the other room, right at Franklin and Jasper's feet.

A stinging mass of fumes rose as glass shattered and the liquids inside combined. Franklin and Jasper began to cough and yell as Marlene slammed the door shut and locked it again.

"Ammonia and bleach, right?" Marlene said as they ran down the hallway toward safety, using Faith's phone as a flashlight.

"Exactly," Faith said. "Any house cleaner knows not to combine the two. They make a deadly gas. In this case, it will slow them down until they get that door unlocked again."

Lights flickered ahead and Faith faltered. "They don't have any other accomplices, do they?"

"Not that I know of," Marlene said. "Besides, isn't that your cat?"

Indeed it was Watson, bolting down the corridor. He gave several loud meows when he saw Faith and leaped into her arms.

She handed the cell phone to Marlene and gathered him close. "What are you doing here, Rumpy? Have you been following me?"

For once, the cat didn't mind his human calling him Rumpy. On her lips, it was the sweetest name in the world—this time. Purring, he rubbed his nose against her cheek, which was almost as soft as his. She was safe and he, Watson, had done his job.

Wolfe Jaxon was next to appear, followed by Officers Rooney, Tobin, and Laddy. "Faith. Marlene. You're all right." Wolfe stopped running, panting. "Thank goodness."

Still holding Watson, Faith laughed. "We are, thanks to Marlene's keys and some old cleaning products."

"What are you talking about?" Wolfe looked puzzled.

Shouts and cries erupted down the corridor, followed by threats. "I think that's your cue," Faith said to the police officers. "Those are the men who killed Doris Lincoln."

The officers exchanged glances and then trotted down the corridor, guns drawn. "Hands up!" Rooney said a moment later. "Right now," Tobin ordered.

"The police? How did the police get down here?" Jasper said, whining.

"It must be your fault," Franklin said. "Listen, officers, this was all his idea."

Faith and the others continued toward the exit. "How did you know to come down here, Wolfe?" Faith asked.

Wolfe nodded at Watson. "Your cat. He carried one of Franklin's business cards in his mouth and laid it at my feet. Then he ran to one of those secret entrances and kept meowing. By then, people realized both Marlene and you were missing." He gave Marlene a sheepish glance. "I thought you kidnapped Faith, along with Franklin."

"I didn't, but it's still all my fault."

"Don't worry about that, Marlene. There were extenuating circumstances." Faith hoped Wolfe would take the whole picture into account and give Marlene another chance.

"I knew about Jasper," Wolfe said softly, "before we hired you."

A series of emotions ran over Marlene's face: fear, dismay, shame, and then, hope. Her shoulders slumped as if the weight of her secret had been lifted. "I'm so sorry, Wolfe. I don't deserve your trust."

He took her arm. "I beg to differ. You've earned it through your excellent work. You were going to turn Franklin and Jasper in, weren't you?"

"I was." Marlene blinked away tears. "I really was."

"Come on, let's get out of here," Wolfe said. "I have hot chocolate and cookies waiting upstairs in my apartment." He extended his other arm to Faith.

"You were pretty confident you'd find us," Faith said with a laugh. She slipped her hand through the crook of his arm.

"I wasn't." Wolfe jerked a thumb at Watson, now padding beside them. "But he was."

The evening's revelations started to sink in and Faith's spirits rose like helium balloons released into the air. Wolfe Jaxon was one of the good guys. Doris Lincoln's killers would be brought to justice. And Faith still had a great job, a lovely place to live, and—most importantly—a brilliant cat who had her back.

What more could a girl want?

After Jasper's and Franklin's confessions, Faith learned that they had been responsible for several troubling incidents. Franklin had stalked her at the retreat and Jasper had broken into her car and assaulted her in the maze. As for Doris Lincoln's belongings, Marlene had produced a key to a storage unit where the trio had stashed her things after the murder. A will was also found, giving the proceeds of her estate to a children's library book fund at the Candle House Library. Eileen was drawing up a list of possible purchases in anticipation of the release of funds from probate.

Faith was standing before her aunt at Candle House Library. "I'm so glad you could help me, Faith." Resting her hands on her hips, Eileen shook her head at the stacks of books overflowing a half dozen long tables. "We've had an incredible amount of donations this year."

Faith tugged Marlene Russell forward. "Eileen, I'd like you to meet Marlene Russell. She's going to help us sort books today. Marlene is the assistant manager at Castleton. Marlene, this is Eileen Piper, my aunt and the librarian here at Candle House Library."

"I've seen you around town," Eileen said with a wide smile. "Welcome."

"Nice to meet you." Marlene almost appeared bashful, Faith noticed. Outside the retreat, she wasn't half as arrogantly assertive. "Where shall we start?"

Eileen pointed. "Over there. We sort by fiction and nonfiction, then organize the nonfiction by subject. Since you're sorting, you get first dibs. Let me know if you want to buy something." She glanced at her watch. "Oh dear! I've got to run a quick errand, but I'll be back soon."

"We'll be fine, Aunt Eileen," Faith said. "Take your time."

"I'll bring back refreshments from the bakery to fortify us." With a wave, Eileen left.

"Do you think we'll find them?" Faith asked Marlene as they began to stack books into piles. Romance went here, how to fix your car or plant a garden went there.

"I hope so. I can't think where else they went." Marlene placed a western on the fiction pile. "Doris told Laura to bring down the discards that Friday before Labor Day."

"And then Doris wasn't around to notice they were gone." Sadness panged at the thought of the librarian. Doris had only been doing her job.

"That's right." Marlene's lips set in a grim line. "I don't think I'll ever forgive myself."

"You're welcome to join Aunt Eileen and me at church this Sunday," Faith said. She knew that God's grace could do what people thought was impossible.

Marlene shrugged. "Maybe I will." She turned a gimlet stare on Faith. "If we're all organized for the incoming retreat, that is."

She's back, Faith thought, hiding a smile and returning to sorting. At the bottom of the pile, a bright red cover winked. Her heart beat a little faster as she quickly dug through to reach it, moving aside a primer on cat training (*Good luck with that!* she thought) and a volume on self-defense (*That might come in handy*).

Faith nudged Marlene. "Look."

Marlene gasped as she picked up *A Study in Scarlet*, seemingly unharmed and still in pristine shape. "Where's the other—oh, here it is." She handed Faith *The Adventures of Sherlock Holmes* identical to the one with the forged signature.

Faith gently opened the front cover. There it was, Sir Arthur Conan Doyle's authentic signature. The Castleton Library collection would be intact once more.

Eileen hurried back into the room. Spotting Marlene and Faith holding the rare volumes, she asked, "Did you find something you want?"

"You could say that, Aunt Eileen." Faith winked at Marlene. "I think they're keepers."